True to Form

True to Form

ELIZABETH BERG

ATRIA BOOKS
New York London Toronto Sydney Singapore

Copyright © 2002 by Elizabeth Berg

ISBN: 0-7434-1134-X

First Atria Books hardcover printing June 2002

10 9 8 7 6 5 4 3 2 1

ATRIA BOOKS is a trademark of Simon & Schuster, Inc.

For information regarding special discounts for bulk purchases, please contact Simon & Schuster Special Sales at 1-800-456-6798 or business@simonandschuster.com

Designed by Jaime Putorti

Printed in the U.S.A.

This book is for that beautiful Asian woman who came to one of my readings in Wellesley, Massachusetts, and asked if I were ever going to write about Katie again. I said I didn't know. She said, "Well, you have to. I have to know what becomes of her."

I think this book will tell you.

Acknowledgments

I am supported in my work by a number of really fine people:

Lisa Bankoff, my stylish and elegantly formidable agent

Patrick Price, her charming assistant, who knows how to do *everything*

Emily Bestler, whose qualities of sensitivity and responsiveness make her an ideal editor

Sarah Branham, her creative assistant

Cathy Lee Gruhn, my fearless publicist

Paolo Pepe, my art director, who so beautifully translates words into images

Phyllis Florin, my best friend, who read this manuscript first and offered honest and valuable criticism

Marianne Quasha, my other best friend, who knows what fabric *really* is

Bill Young, my sweetie, who makes daily life more joyful than I had ever imagined it could be

Last, but certainly not least: The friends I've made here in the great city of Chicago, where I've finally found home.

True to Form

I T IS THE FIRST SUNDAY EVENING of the summer, the sky an ash rose color and losing its light to night. I am sitting on the floor in my room with a mirror propped up against a stack of magazines, setting my hair according to the directions in *Modern Style*. If I do it right, I will get a perfect flip. I just need to sleep in such a way that the rollers do not become pushed out of place, as they usually do. Either they get pushed out of place or I take them all out in the middle of the night. I don't know why. I don't even remember doing it, I just wake up and there the rollers are, thrown down on the floor. I guess my sleep self and my awake self don't agree about beauty.

The radio is turned on low to "Moody River," and my question is, Why did she kill herself if the guy was just a friend? And also, how can Pat Boone be singing so smoothly if his heart is broken? He sounds like Perry Como singing "Magic Moments" when he should be sounding like Brenda Lee sobbing, "I'm sorry, sooo sorry."

I am thinking about how tomorrow I will lie out on a towel in the yard, slicked up with baby oil to get going on my tan. I like it when you lie there for a long time and feel the sun's heat like a red thing behind your lids. You see a map of your own veins, and then when you open your eyes the view is bleached a bit of its colors. When I was nine years old someone told me you must never look at the sun straight on because it could make you blind. This made me

1

go right outside and stare up at it, and when my eyes protested and shut automatically, I held my lids open until my eyes burned and watered so much I had to stop. I did not go blind. I do have to wear glasses, but I was wearing them before I stared at the sun. I am this way, sometimes, that I just have to find things out for myself.

I have a feeling percolating under my skin that says this will be a really important summer. Just a feeling that doesn't go away. I think sometimes I am a little psychic, like my grandmother who could read tea leaves. She would sit at the kitchen table with her beautiful white hair up in a bun, and she would be wearing an apron that sagged over her bosom like another bosom. She would stare into the cup for a long time, and nobody talked; even the air seemed to hold still. Then she would look up, and her blue eyes would seem clearer and not quite her own. She would settle her shoulders, and, in a low and intimate voice, tell people things about their lives. I thought for a long time she was a gypsy queen, but my mind just made that up; she was really just a woman from England who married my grandfather from Ireland. She was a housewife who made good gravy and kept a parakeet in her kitchen.

Once, when I was in third grade, my grandmother read tea leaves for me. My mother was there, and her sisters, my aunts Rose and Betty, were there, too. I remember I was so nervous I sat under the kitchen table, and my grandmother had to tell me things without looking at me. She said I had a boyfriend, which was true, Billy Harris was his name, and I got all embarrassed even though no one could see me. Then she told me he liked me too, which was not so true, since if you asked him, "Do you like Katie Nash?" he would have said, "Who?"

I miss my aunts a lot. Since my mother died a couple of years ago, I never see them anymore. We used to go and visit for a week or so every summer. Rose was very prim and proper, but full of a warm love. When I used to stay there, my cousins and I washed up for bed at night in a dishpan at the kitchen sink, and Aunt Rose made sure we got our ears good. Ivory soap, she used, those floating cakes bigger than a kid's whole hand. She made plain dinners but they were the kind of food a person always enjoys. Like just meat loaf from the recipe on the back of the oatmeal box, served with mashed potatoes, butter filling the little well in the middle, and some green beans from the can, all served on an embroidered table-cloth. Her sheets smelled like outside, and everybody used to say you could eat from her kitchen floor. I used to think, *Why would you want to do that?* and I would imagine my uncle Harry sitting there cross-legged with his napkin tucked into his shirt, leaning over awkwardly to lift his scrambled eggs from the linoleum.

Aunt Betty was a wild woman, that's what she called herself. She told me she was engaged to another man when my uncle Jim proposed to her. She wore a lot of makeup and smoked constantly and painted her fingernails and toenails blood red. She and my uncle were very social, and I never saw anyone look as glamorous as she did when they went out. She would wake up her children for a meteor shower or a good sunrise, and she was always asking them to tell her things they learned in school; she thought her children were wonderful. Every Sunday morning, she would make Monkey Bread, and there was always enough for everyone.

My dad doesn't want to visit my aunts anymore. I guess he has a new life now with my stepmother, Ginger, and the aunts just don't figure in. Sometimes I get mail from them: a joke card from Betty; a card with Jesus on it from Rose. They both call me Honey, which makes for an inside curl of pleasure. I thought I would always go and see them, every summer.

Well, you never know what life will turn out to be. Sometimes when I lie in bed at night, I think of bad things that can happen and how much we can never know, and it's so scary. It's like taking the lid off a box that's in front of you all the time, but usually you leave it alone. But every now and then, you take the lid off and you look in and the box is so dark and deep and full of writhing possibilities it gives you the shivers.

I lean back against my bed, let out a big breath, and look around my bedroom. I am used to it now, which probably means it's about time to move. Every time I get used to something, it's time to leave it. "We have orders," my father will say, and that's that, we're on the way to wherever the army tells us to go.

I like this room. It feels more private than any place I've ever had, situated the way it is at the end of the hall. If my sister, Diane, were still living with us, she would have gotten this room; she always got the best room. But she lives by herself in California now, because she ran away when she was eighteen. We talk about twice a month, and once in a while she comes to visit, but mostly it is just no good between her and my father; it never was. My father was always fierce, but after my mother died it seemed like he got a lot worse. And Diane finally just left. He never talks about it, but I know he is sorry. One thing my stepmother has done is to make my father a little softer, not so mean. It's odd; I think he loved my mother more, but he treats Ginger better. And I think I know why. It is because she is not as nice to him as my mother was. She pushes back, sometimes. She draws a line and says don't you cross this. Now you tell me why someone is nicer to the person who treats him worse.

My favorite place in my room is my desk drawer. In it is a little figure of a bird all covered with jewels. I don't think they're real jewels, but maybe they are. It was given to me by a boy I did not know, for no reason. It was a while ago, just after my mother had died, and I was sitting out by myself in the middle of a field on a summer day, and the boy appeared out of nowhere. He was younger than I, I thought—smaller, at least, and so I wasn't afraid. I said, "Hey," and he said nothing back. "What are you doing?" I asked, and again he said nothing. I asked him if he spoke English, and he just smiled and shrugged. I stared at him for a while, and then I patted the ground. He sat next to me, his knees drawn up under his chin, and together we watched the movement of the breeze through the tall weeds, the lazy shifting of the gigantic cumulus clouds that filled the sky that day, and, once, the magical hovering of a dragonfly, colored metallic blue. We only pointed at things, but it was a good conversation. We sat for a good fifteen or twenty minutes, and then the boy got up to leave. But first he took the bird out of his pocket and gave it to me. I was amazed by his generosity, but I am ashamed to say that I made no move at all to refuse that gift. It is the main thing in my drawer, because it was a miracle and it came without asking. Sometimes when I think of that boy, I think, Wait, was he mute? And sometimes I think—the thought very small and private— Was he an angel? And sometimes I think, in a way that makes me feel like bawling, Was he my mother? That thought is the smallest and most private of all, and it lives in my heart, and it will never be told to anyone.

Also in my drawer is a photo of baby pigs. I remember them vaguely from a time we lived on a farm in Indiana. I think I was three. I remember being barefoot, standing on the wooden rail of a fence, looking down at those pigs. I wanted them to be my dollies; I wanted to wheel them in a carriage, put bonnets on their heads, feed them from bottles, and cover them when they slept. But they were not babies, they were pigs. So I only watched them lie by their mother in their neat, pink row; and I watched them take their grunty little steps around the sty.

I have some rocks I cracked open and kept for their gorgeous insides. I have some acorns, because look what comes from them. I have a pressed flower, a rose I would still call pink, even though its edges have turned tea-colored. I have pictures of beautiful things cut out of magazines: a willow tree next to a river, a kitchen lit up by morning sun, a monarch on a red poppy, a herd of sheep on a hill in Ireland, a wooden, straight-back chair positioned by a window with a blowing white curtain. I have a lot of pictures of dogs, too. I would like to have seven dogs.

I have something that I drew, a woman's face that is full of sorrow. And it looks like a real picture that an artist did. It looks that way to me. And the thing is, I don't know how to draw. I was sitting at my desk one day, my head in my hands, and I had that middle ache that is just the pain that comes with being alive sometimes, that kind of personal despair. I don't know why it comes, but I know it used to get my mother too. Every once in a while, she would sit so still, her hands in her lap, and she would have a little smile on her face that was not really a smile. What's wrong? I once asked, and she looked up quickly and she saw that I saw. After that, she would usually close herself in her bedroom until it was over—it never took that long, really. She didn't like for anyone to see her that way. She didn't want anyone to know.

But I had that same kind of feeling one day, that veil of sadness between me and the world, and I had a piece of paper in front of me and I drew that woman's face like I was in a dream, like someone else was borrowing my hand. And I have never shown it to anyone, and I have never drawn anything good since then, either.

Lately, I have begun writing a lot more poems, and I have been saving them in my drawer. And it's funny, the same thing happens, about someone else borrowing my hand. I get a feeling; I step off into space; and a thing makes up itself.

I have red lipstick in my drawer that was my mother's, with the mark of her mouth on it. I have a rhinestone button I found outside, feathers from birds, pennies that mean good luck. I have a box of crayons that I intend never to use, I just like to look at them all perfect and read the names of the colors out loud, and I like to smell them deep, like I smell the test papers at school that have just come off the mimeograph machine. I have some torn-out hairdos that I would like to get, if my hair will ever grow really long instead of acting paralyzed.

Sometimes I think, What if I died and someone looked in my drawer? I wonder what they would understand about me. Probably not so much—for one thing, they would get the crayons wrong. I think, actually, that none of us understands anyone else very well, because we're all too shy to show what matters the most. If you ask me, it's a major design flaw. We ought to be able to say, Here, look what I am. I think it would be quite a relief.

EVERY YEAR I DO THIS. Every year I go outside to tan for the first time and I know I'm only supposed to do fifteen minutes a side, but then I think, Oh, maybe a little more, and then a little more, and then I see the redness and I know I'm in for it. I come inside and take a cold shower, but no, it is too late. I am cooked.

It is Monday morning and I am lying in bed with no clothes on because that's how much it hurts, I can't even wear clothes. Ginger didn't say anything because that's the kind of person she is. My father came to stand in my doorway and look at me before he went to work, and he moved his mouth like he was shifting a toothpick from one side to the other. Finally, "When are you going to learn?" he asked, and I shrugged. Which hurt, because my shoulders are the worst.

"How long were you out there?" he asked, and I mumbled something.

"What's that?" he asked.

"About twenty minutes."

"And you got burned like that?"

"Maybe it was thirty. Or a little more. It *might* have been forty, but I don't *think* so." It was an hour, said the angel on my shoulder, and the devil said, *Shut up!*

He shook his head and said, again, "When are you going to learn?"

I just nodded. There was no answer. But then he knew that. He called Ginger, and when she came up to him he jerked his head toward me and said, "Take care of her, will you?" His tenderness, in its usual disguise. Ginger looked at me, a message in her eyes, and I stared back, I know.

The first thing I do after he leaves is call my friend Cynthia to come over. I know she will read aloud to me from *True Romance,* or hold up movie magazine pictures, or play the records I ask her to put on. At lunch time she will make the sandwiches we like and bring one to me: baloney and lots and lots of mayonnaise on white bread with lettuce and potato chips on there too. I am sorry to say that one of the biggest reasons we are friends is that we are both sort of losers. The only good thing about that is you can do certain things like the sandwiches and who cares.

ONE THING I DO NOT UNDERSTAND about parents is how out of their mouths come two different things at almost exactly the same time. They are the true forked-tongue people of the world.

Here is my father talking to me at the breakfast table this morning: "Katie, you're thirteen years old. You're really growing up, now, and I think it's time you started working in the summers." No complaint from me so far. A lift in my chest of pure happiness, in fact, that inside yip. Because one thing I would love is to have a job, maybe at the concession stand at the swimming pool where lifeguards join the crowd in asking for a Nutty Buddy. They stand so handsome and nonchalant, their whistle lying in the little valley of their chest, zinc oxide on their noses, their eyes sexy behind their sunglasses. Oftentimes they take a dip before they come to the concession stand and you can see the little rivers of water zigzag down their hairy legs. Their faces look like boys', but their legs look like men, which gives you the inside shivers.

Some of the lifeguards have actually saved lives, have knelt beside a bluish body and made it breathe again. I saw part of that one time. I was on the outside of a thick circle of people gathered around someone the lifeguards had pulled out of the pool. He was a fat man, and all I could see was one of his arms, lying useless beside him. But then he got saved. An ambulance came, the crowd parted,

10

and he was carried off on a stretcher with a red blanket over him, an oxygen mask over his face. I remember thinking, If it were me, I'd be embarrassed about the oxygen mask. But the man wasn't embarrassed. I guess he was in shock, his eyes all blank. I watched him pass by and I thought, For the rest of his life, he will tell this story, *I wanted to go swimming.*

Anyway, if you work at a pool, you can develop a personal relationship with the lifeguards and get your own money to buy things besides. But working at the pool is not going to be my job. Because what my father said next is, "There is an elderly couple two blocks over who need help for a few hours on Mondays, Wednesdays, and Fridays. And I know Mrs. Wexler is looking for a sitter for her kids a couple of days a week, as well."

There is this sense of powerlessness that comes to me sometimes, and it makes my chest feel paralyzed, and it makes my stomach feel like someone is wringing it out. That feeling came to me then. I knew it was all over and there was nothing, nothing, nothing I could do, especially with my father who sometimes gets mad if you only say "But . . ." Still, I tried. I made my face blank as a white towel, and I said, "My job is going to be baby-sitting?" Mrs. Wexler lives two doors down and has three kids, ages six, seven, and eight. All boys. I've baby-sat for her a few times. Trust me that it is not the kind of job you would say is fun. Or grown-up. I felt like standing in front of a wall and punching it again and again, but instead I had a little smile on my face, and I moved only to tuck my hair politely behind my ears.

"You're to start next Monday," my father said.

"But . . . baby-sitting for a *couple?*"

"Yes." He stood and looked at his watch. "The wife is apparently quite ill. They need some help."

Oh great, I thought, and right away I got an idea of how that place would be. I got the smell in my nose of the place. No offense, but when you're around older people there is a smell, even when they're not sick. It is like old closet smell. Not the thing you want to be around in the summer, when everywhere else is suntan lotion and grass clippings. Plus old people always keep their houses dark and they are kind of cheap about food. I have been invited inside old people's houses, and when they ask if you would like some cookies, what they give you is two Vanilla Wafers or a Fig Newton on a saucer that is not the cleanest thing you've ever seen. It's not their fault, I'm not saying that, but I just so much do *not* want to be a *baby-sitter* for my summer job.

Here is how much my opinion counts: Zero. My opinion is called talking back. I can say things to my stepmother. Ginger will listen to anything, the calm look in her eyes a welcome mat to your feelings. But she would not be able to help me on this one. I was doomed for the whole rest of the summer, starting right at that very minute. It wasn't fair. And it wasn't right.

"Tonight, I'll show you where they live," my father said. "Introduce you."

"Okay," I said.

My father kissed Ginger quickly on the mouth, and left. The screen door slammed. The car door slammed. The engine started. Next came the low whine of the car in reverse, backing out of the driveway. A pause, while he shifted gears. Gone.

So now I am lying on my bed with my door closed at ten in the morning, like I am a sick old person myself. I know if I went outside there would be the cheer-up sight of roses in gardens and clouds puffed up in the sky like they are pure proud of themselves. Little kids riding their bikes down the street full of the freedom of no homework. But I don't want to be cheered up until I am done with feeling mad. Here comes Ginger down the hall with the vacuum cleaner, which shows no respect at all.

I open my door and stand there, my arms crossed. She looks up, turns off the vacuum. "What is it?"

"Nothing."

"Can I come in?" This is one thing I like about Ginger, that she does not assume your room is hers just because she is the woman of the house. I stand aside, and she comes in and sits on my wrinkled bed. I sit at my desk and get the bright *zing!* that I don't have to do homework here for a long time, but that is of no help at the moment.

"You're feeling bad about working?" She has her hair up in a French twist, some spit curls on either side. She wears a peach-colored housedress, tight at the waist. Loafers. As for me, I am still in my shorty pajamas. They do not look on me the way they looked on the model in the Sears catalog.

"I want to work," I say. "But baby-sitting is not a real job."

"Why not?"

"Because it's . . ." I shrug, look down. There are my fat knees.

"You get paid, right?"

"Yes."

"Well, that's a job. You do some work and you are paid. And you know, when you are thirteen, your choices *are* somewhat limited."

"But who wants to be a baby-sitter? Especially for old people!"

"I can understand your feelings. But I think you might like the Randolphs. They're very nice."

"How do you know them?"

"Your father and I see Mr. Randolph when we take our walks after dinner. He's got a garden he likes to putter in. And he always comes over to say hello to us, and to pet the dogs. Last night, he told us he needed some help, and your dad volunteered your services."

"But he didn't ask me."

"No. You're right. He did not."

"Not that he ever does."

"Well. Not often enough. I agree with you there."

We stare at each other. Finally, I say, "Can I ask you something?"

"Of course."

"How can you . . . why do you like my dad so much?"

She smiles. "Well. You know he's not nearly as tough as he acts."

"Yes, but . . ."

She comes over to me, puts her hand on my shoulder in a way that I like. "I guess it's what I've told you before, I like a challenge. I always have liked men that others find difficult."

I think of the last time my father took Ginger out for dinner, how the clothes she was going to wear were lined up on her bed while she was in the shower, singing. Her blue crepe dress, her lacy slip, her nylon stockings. Her high heels on the floor, dusted with baby powder and waiting for her to step into them. I think of how he put his hand to the small of her back as they walked out the door together that night. He is a scary man, but she finds other things. I guess this is her thrill.

"For you . . . ," Ginger says. "Well, I know it can be awfully hard." She bends down, looks me in the eye. "But you know what? He loves you, Katie. Oh, he really does."

I swallow hard. One thing I hate is crying in the morning.

"You do know that, right?" Ginger asks, and I nod. Then I say, small, "But I wish he would do it different."

"I know you do. I wish he would, too. I wish he would be easier on you. I think he is getting better, but it will take a while for him to . . . In the meantime, I want you to know that you can come to me, Katie. For anything."

I draw a circle on my knee with my finger. I hear the ticking of my bedside alarm clock, the rumble of a truck going down the street outside. My mother is so far away, she is too far away forever.

Ginger straightens, kisses the top of my head. "How about some breakfast?" And I nod, because there is nothing else to be done. You might as well eat. I'll give Bridgett my toast crusts and then take her out in the yard to play ball with her; it's not her fault.

Bones will lie sleeping in the sun as usual; that's all he ever does when I take him out. He's probably as old as Mr. Randolph in dog years.

So this is the beginning of my glamorous summer. It doesn't matter that I'm only thirteen; even if I were seventeen, I would still have to do what he says. Would you like to work at Famous Barr and see the latest clothes for fall? Oh, no thank you, I'm going to baby-sit. Would you like to work at Dairy Queen and get to see the long lines outside your little window while you make the curl on top of every cone? Oh, no thanks, I would much rather baby-sit. Would you like to come to Hollywood and be the assistant to Rock Hudson and Doris Day and get paid a thousand dollars a day? Oh, certainly not, not when I can hang around some house that isn't mine playing wrestling match with three boys from hell.

SAY SANTA CLAUS WENT ON A SEVERE DIET: Bingo, Mr. Randolph. There he is before me with twinkly blue eyes and a mouth that really is like a bow. White hair and a white beard. But skinny as can be, with his shirt tucked into his pants and sort of drowning there. His suspenders ought to be paid double for the work they're doing. "Hi, nice to meet you," I said, when we were introduced, but what I felt like saying is, "Whoa! Did anybody ever tell you you looked like someone?"

"Ah, *Katie!*" he says, stepping aside from the door. "I'm so happy to meet you. Won't you come in?"

He leads us into the living room, which is a really nice room, two blue sofas with lots of triangle pillows on them. A couple of comfy chairs and a fireplace. Pictures on the wall in gold frames and nice drapes held back fancy. He points to one of the sofas and says, "Have a seat."

I sit at the edge of the sofa with one foot tucked behind the other, which is how you're supposed to so you don't show what's up your skirt even when you're wearing shorts, which, of course, it being summer, I am. My father sits beside me, his big hands in his lap.

Mr. Randolph clears his throat, and I all of a sudden get that panicked feeling because what if I'm the one who is supposed to say something first. But then Mr. Randolph says, "I guess your father must have told you what I'm looking for."

I look at my father, who is staring straight ahead. I am on my own. "Yes, sir. He said you had a wife who was sick and you needed some help."

"That's right. Elsie has been ill for some time, and it's gotten difficult for me to take care of her by myself. What I need is some help bathing her, preparing meals, and maybe you could read to her a bit when I run out for errands."

"Oh, okay," I say, though what I am feeling is, *Oh, no*.

"Why don't we go and see her?" Mr. Randolph asks.

My father stands as though he's going to go with us, but then he all of a sudden says, "I'll tell you what, I believe I'll just let the three of you talk. Katie, I'll see you back at home, all right?"

Mr. Randolph looks a little surprised, but I think I know why my father is doing this. I think he is remembering my mother lying sick in bed before she died, and the memory is like holding something too hot.

"Okay, Dad." I smile at Mr. Randolph like I am fine-and-dandy ready to meet his wife, even though I would rather be doing math. We make our way down a hall and into a bedroom, and what do I come face-to-face with but Mrs. Randolph's hiney. She is lying on her side, the covers pulled off, and her blue nightgown is hiked up clear to her shoulder blades. I have never seen an adult's hiney in real life, except once a part of Ginger's when I accidentally opened the bathroom door on her. Hers did not look like this. This is a hiney like a balloon all deflated. And there is Mrs. Randolph's knobby backbone and her hair all white and see-through sticking out all around her head like she has her finger in the socket. I take a step back. In my mind, I see my room, all my normal things waiting for me when I get home.

Mr. Randolph rushes forward and gently pulls the nightgown down and the sheet up. And the whole time he's doing it, he is talking in such a dignified voice, saying, "There we go. That's better." He straightens, clasps his hands before him. "Now. Dear? We have a visitor. I'd like you to meet our neighbor, Katie."

Sometimes it seems like a little moment brings a whole world with it. I mean that I see Mr. Randolph cover up his wife like she is made of thin glass, and I hear him speak in a voice so kind and low but also full of a shy pain, and all of a sudden I really want to help him. Mr. Randolph has no fear of showing how much he loves someone, even though she is pure disgusting. I saw this kind of thing once before, when I was on my way into a store, and coming out was this really big kid sitting in a wheelchair. He was drooling and all twisted up like a human pretzel, and he was making a sound between moaning and laughing. I saw that kid and I felt scared of him and also sort of sick to my stomach as I looked at him, looking up at me. Then I saw how his mother leaned down and spoke to him and very gently wiped at his face with her flowered hanky and I felt so ashamed. I remember I watched her wheel him away, his head bent to the side all strange, and he was just her son with a crewcut like the other boys. I got tears in my eyes, but they were not the crying kind, they were just the kind that show you your body agrees so much with what your mind just said.

"Elsie?" Mr. Randolph says, and a little sound comes out of the Mrs.

"It's Katie, the girl I told you about," he says, and Mrs. Randolph turns over. "Oh! Hello," she says, and her voice sounds crackly, like a bad phone connection. She doesn't smile. She looks like the FBI photos at the post office.

I shrug. "Hello."

"Can you come closer?" she asks.

I walk up to the bedside, one of my hands holding the other tightly, and she stares into my face. "Aren't you nice," she says, and I don't have any idea what to say back.

"Sweetheart, can you get my glasses?" she asks, and Mr. Randolph digs in the drawer in the bedside stand and carefully puts them on her. "Ah," she says, "Now." She looks at me again, and then she does smile, and her face looks almost pretty; you can see how she maybe used to be.

One thing I feel bad about is her glasses are all greasy. When I am the one taking care of her, first I'll wash her glasses. It's odd, but when I think of that, I start to get kind of excited about the job. I get an idea that on the way here next time, I'll pick a little bouquet of flowers she can keep on her bedside to remind her that no matter what, those flowers are still there. Maybe I can take her outside to see them—there's a wheelchair all folded up over in the corner. But first things first. I shake her hand, with all her veins sticking out like little blue roads, and when she says, Are you going to be coming over to relieve my darling Henry? I say, Yes ma'am, I am.

BEFORE I GO TO SLEEP I like to listen to the transistor radio. I put the volume on low and let it rest over my ear. Sometimes I fall asleep like that. Tonight I am listening to Fab Freddy, as usual. He's the deejay I like best. He has such a friendly attitude, and I like it when he talks to people—you can call in and he actually puts you on the air. Once I tried calling, but then I hung up before he got to me. I started getting a chest ache, waiting for him to say, "HI! You're on KOOL radio, with Fab Freddy! What's happening, baaaaaaby?"

Tonight Freddy is saying, "Don't forget, now, next Friday night between nine and ten P.M., we'll be announcing the winner of our 'Trip of a Lifetime' contest! Send us a postcard with your name, address, and phone number. If we announce your name, all you have to do is pick up the phone and call us, and TWA will send you to the *city of your choice!* So get those postcards in here. Remember, only one entry per person."

My eyelids pop open like cartoon window shades. No way could I win, but if I did, I know where I'd go: back to Texas, where I moved here from. I would really like, for once in my life, to go back to a place I used to live, which I have never been able to do. Sometimes it seems like I just made those places up. Also, I would like to see my friend, Cherylanne, one more time. We are not as close as we used to be, but I would like to see her anyway, because unbelievable things are happening to her.

I get out of bed, write, ENTER CONTEST!!! on a piece of paper and put it smack in the middle of my desk. Then, from the back of my drawer, I pull out a letter from Cherylanne, sent to me about a month ago. I'll read it again to get her fresh in my mind, just in case.

I prop up both of my pillows so that I can lean against them and read in the luxury way, and begin.

Dear Katie,

You are going to flat out die when you hear what is happening with me. I, Cherylanne, am completely in love with the boy I am going to marry and soon. His name is Darren McGovern and you never met him, he just moved here. Instant attraction is what it was, and with one thing leading to the other, all I can say is, picture me in white. I have not told one soul about the marry part except you, not even Darren, but when it is meant to be, it is meant to be. I am so excited I can hardly sleep at night, wondering where we will live as man and wife and all the other things such as how many children will we have and also of course the intimacy part. Some girls have told me it hurts so much like a broomstick through a keyhole but they are just guessing unless they are more sluts than I thought. Anyway, here's what I'll bet you are dying to know: black hair, blue eyes, and tall, tall, tall. His own car and he can sing and accompany himself on guitar. Elvis is probably what you're thinking and you are just about right! If you still lived here, you could see him when he picks me up but that was not meant to be.

Well, there is not much else news here. I know I haven't written back very much, but I did want you to know how I finally turned out. I looked on the map where Missouri was, so you know I have thought of you. Also, I thought of you because I now have completed my move into all different makeup, and I

21

know how you relied on me for tips. It is too long to tell you everything now, but trust me that I am more now on the side of elegant like Jackie. One tip I will pass on right away: Do not fall for lip gloss that has a taste like green apple. Neither you nor you-know-who will like it. Do you have a you-know-who? Or does your heart still weep for Jimmy? Sometimes that happens that your one love in life is a tragedy, and if it has happened to you, I am so sorry, it must be très, très painful. I have to go now.

Love,

Cherylanne

Jimmy. The gas station attendant I loved so much, even if he was ten years older than I and married too. I haven't thought of him for a long time. Now when I do, I see that the pain I used to feel has transformed itself into something else, something kind of holy and put away. He was my first love and will always be, but in time I think there will be another. That is one lesson I finally learned from him.

I fold up Cherylanne's letter, slide it under my pillow. Then I arrange my arms and legs just right for sleep. Sometimes when I do that, I think there is nothing wrong in the whole world. I think it is how my dogs feel, too, when they lie down and sigh loud out their noses.

I ONCE HEARD SOMEONE SAY that it is a sin to wish for time to go faster, but that person has never sat in the living room of the Wexler house watching three boys try to kill each other. What we have here is Mark, Henry, and David rolled together in a ball in the middle of the floor. They are the Three Stooges, they said, and now no matter how hard I have tried I cannot stop them from yelling "Chowderhead!" and trying to poke one another's eyes out, they just keep going. Everybody knows the Three Stooges are only kidding, but not these kids, they really mean it. I am flat-out exhausted and have finally collapsed on the couch to just watch them. When their mother comes home I will say there are David's eyeballs, which your other son, Mark, popped out. I don't care anymore.

And then, just like that, they stop. They just sit there looking at me like I am the entertainment lady with the whistle around her neck. I wish I could send them outside, but no, it's raining hard.

"Are you finished?" I ask.

Nothing. Just Henry scratching a line of mosquito bites on his arm about six miles long. He is the littlest one, not only in age but also he's just little. His ears stick out and he wears glasses and his hair stands up in back from a cowlick worse than mine. He is exactly between cute and tragic. If it were only Henry and me, we might have good time, but we have his two older brothers, who look like twins, but aren't. They have the same dark hair and narrow eyes and mean expressions and heavy builds. They never look at you straight on, and they are always grinning a little like they have a secret from you. A secret like, Watch out if you sit down, because there is a good chance there will be a surprise if you do. I have already sat on the whoopee cushion, and when I did, they all did a little dance of congratulations to themselves, even Henry.

"Your mother will be home in an hour," I say, and I can feel those sixty long minutes pressing down on me, taking away my breathing space. "We can play Crazy Eights or we can make cookies."

Well, I have to say I have just surprised myself, saying the cookies part. I don't really know if Mrs. Wexler would like me to do that. When I came, she was sitting at the kitchen table, painting her fingernails. Her hair was done nicely in a flip and sprayed to stay that way, and she was wearing a blue skirt and a fancy white blouse, white high-heel sandals, and pearl earrings. I thought she looked so nice to just go grocery shopping. It only goes to show you how having animals for sons can make you desperate enough to dress up like the queen of Sheba when all you're doing is going to get more Oxydol. I am having girls, and then only one.

While Mrs. Wexler waited for her nails to dry, I sat at the kitchen table to listen to my instructions, which were basically to let them eat lunch whenever they were ready—peanut butter and jelly sandwiches—and if it stopped raining to get them out of the house. Which I would do by myself, of course. Then Mrs. Wexler all of a sudden said, "Do you have a boyfriend, Katie?" I felt myself blush a little as I said no. "Well," she said, "don't be in any hurry." She smiled a bitter smile and said, "I've been with my husband since junior high school. Isn't that sweet." Then she stopped smiling and just stared at me like I wasn't there. But after a second she snapped out of it, leaped up, and grabbed her purse, yelled, "You boys be*have!*" and was gone. And her sons began their favorite game of all time; torture the baby-sitter.

But now, "Cookies! Cookies! Cookies!" they are yelling, and they are all jumping up and down. I hold up my hand and yell even louder than them, "ANYONE WHO IS JUMPING UP AND DOWN MAY NOT HELP WITH THE MAKING OF THE COOKIES, OR THE EATING OF THEM!"

Stop. Not one movement on the part of any of them, though I can see David and Mark looking at each other, trying to plan something using the language of the eyebrows. One eyebrow up. *Should we?* Two eyebrows down: *No, better not.* I have never been one to yell, but I can see now that there might be times when it's good.

"Now," I say, in the calm and knowing voice of a teacher. "Let's go and see if we have what we need. Let's find the ingredients." I start for the kitchen. I am walking so straight and tall three books would stay balanced on top of my head. Only Henry follows me. Mark and David are standing frozen, pretending they are statues. I never saw kids so quick to make a dumb game out of everything.

"What kind shall we make?" I ask Henry, loudly, and just as I suspected, that gets the other two to come slamming into the kitchen. They would never let Henry decide anything.

"Chocolate chip!" David yells, and Mark yells, "Yeah, chocolate dootie!"

Now they are jumping around the kitchen and I am looking in the cupboards for chocolate chips and wishing I were at home, asleep, in the middle of the night. Lo and behold, there they are, chocolate chips, lying right beside a box of Minute Rice. I hope it's okay to use them, but I don't care if it isn't. It's use up the chips or have the mother come home to kids with no eyes and a baby-sitter dead from trying.

"ANYONE WHO DOES NOT SIT DOWN AT THE KITCHEN TABLE WILL BE EXPELLED FROM THE KITCHEN," I say. And they sit down. They are actually quiet for

about three seconds. And in those three seconds I see that Mark
has big circles under his eyes, and it makes me all of a sudden kind
of tender for him. I start to think that maybe I can get things to go
smoother; it is all a matter of child psychology. When Mark reaches
over and starts punching David, I try something. I say, "Mark, I
think you would be good at the mashing butter part, you look like a
very intelligent young man." Bingo. He looks at me like I have
anointed him king of the world. I have to hold my head down to
keep my triumph in before Mark sees it and goes back to being a
jerk.

FRIDAY MORNING. Tonight, kids will be going out on dates to the movies like crazy, but I will be going with Cynthia, as usual. I wonder sometimes what it really is that makes some kids popular and some kids losers. I wonder if you are born one way or another and, no matter what, you can never change it. I see those advice columns, and books like 'Twixt Twelve and Twenty, and they make it sound like all you have to do is sit down in front of your mirror and have a little talk with yourself, and presto, you are different. Happy and good-looking, with people drawn to you everywhere you go. First of all, I don't even have a mirror in my room. I use the bathroom mirror. I can just see myself locking the door and standing in there to look into my own eyes, trying to change into a popular person, and there it would be, a knock on the door. My father, Are you about done in there?

Cherylanne once told me it matters a lot who you hang around with, that if you get seen with losers, people will just naturally think you're one too. Which is why I was not allowed to hang around with her except in the neighborhood; I couldn't be with her in our school. At the time, it didn't matter to me, I was just so glad to be with her sometimes. She was one of those really pretty girls who seem to just know so much, with so many beautiful things in her closet and about three hundred bottles of perfume. Now I understand more about her, and I am aware that she doesn't know nearly as much as she thinks

27

she does; in fact, she's kind of stupid. But she might have been right about hanging around with losers; it only makes you worse.

But how can you get popular one day, when the day before you were not? It is not just clothes and makeup, although that helps. It is not good looks, although that helps even more. It is something else; it is that thing where people just want to have something of you, or be like you, you are just so interesting or something. I really don't get it. Hands all around me reach in and pull out prizes; I come up empty every time; where did you find that?

But even losers have boyfriends—loser boyfriends, but boy-friends just the same. I wonder when my time of having a boyfriend will come, and no matter what Mrs. Wexler says, I wish it would be soon. It's okay to go out with your girlfriend, but if you go on a Friday night you feel stupid in front of all the date people. Sometimes a couple right in front of you will start kissing, and then you feel bad to look at them, but you have to.

Fifteen more minutes until I have to leave for the Randolphs'. I sit at my desk and look through my drawer to kill some time. I have been thinking about this poetry, haiku. It is like a clean and sunny white room, nothing in it, so you can see the sun better. In the library was a whole book of it, which I did not bring home because I didn't want even myself to know I wanted to try. But last night I got a clean new notebook, and on the cover I put a fake Japanese symbol. I made a kind of F with a box in it, and some furls around it. I did my first try at haiku, which is a perfect name for what it is. Now I open the notebook and read:

> *Sheets stuck to my legs*
> *The top of my head on fire*
> *Summer sits on me*

Well. The only thing good is, it's the right number of syllables. I don't know why I thought it was good last night, when the truth is it's really terrible. Whoa. It is a true embarrassment when you feel shy in front of your own self, and that is just exactly what I feel now. Still, I am willing to try again, because the thing about writing poetry is you can throw away lots of things and then all of a sudden you feel like your pen has turned golden. It might help to switch to winter, and also this time not think so much. I close my eyes tight for a moment, then open them and write.

> *White snow covers tan*
> *It looks to me like crumb cake*
> *Nourishment for eyes*

Well, this is no better, and anyway, it's almost time to go to work. When you're a poet, you never get enough time to write poetry, so I might as well get used to it. Once a real poet came to school to talk to us. She was so exciting because she looked just like a beatnik with her long, black hair and such black rings around her eyes and also all black clothes and leather sandals like Jesus. She read us three poems that were so beautiful, and then it was time for questions. One kid asked what her real job was, and she said her real job was writing poems, but in order to afford her real job, she worked as a telephone operator. Which right away showed me to never think anything you see is the only thing it is. It made me sorry to think that someone who could write a poem that could give you the chills had to spend so many long hours a day saying, "Operator." But in another way it made me happy to know that things can be so surprising. Like the waitress who gives you the hamburger might also be a painter. And Lana Turner, the sweater girl, who was serving up ice cream sodas in Hollywood when she got discovered. This is one of my favorite things to imagine: The man comes in and puts his hat down on the counter, and orders a root beer float. And then he watches Lana make it with his eyes sort of squinty. Suddenly he stands up and shouts, "Come with me, young lady! I'm going to make you a star!" And Lana takes off her apron and inside her fireworks of the heart are exploding. On her way out, she says, "Hey, Al? I quit."

Sometimes I think, What if something like that ever happened to me? What would I do? Probably I would be afraid. Probably I would say to the man, "That's okay, thanks anyway." You have to be willing to take chances. You have to not be so afraid. That is the first step to getting anywhere.

After I comb my hair into the shortest ponytail in the universe, I rip the haikus I did into long shreds and put them in my wastebasket. This is also what I do with drawings I don't like. Or ones that I shouldn't have done in the first place. Once I drew breasts and a penis. You can bet I covered them over with scribbles before I ripped them up. The devil said, *Why don't you draw some breasts and a penis, huh? How would that be, to just draw two huge breasts and a big fat penis?* The angel covered her mouth and gasped. Then she said, all smug, *You wouldn't do that, would you, Katie?* But I did. The whole time I was drawing there was a spreading warmth inside me that started you know where. It was quite a shock. But it was a pleasure, too. The angel smacked her forehead. The devil raised his pitchfork and danced.

MR. RANDOLPH IS HOLDING MRS. RANDOLPH on her side and I am washing her back. This is while she is in bed, believe it or not, and so it requires a certain skill, like you have to be careful not to knock the pan of water into the bed. The pan is a big pan, like you boil spaghetti in, but now there's water mixed with some bath oil. Rose-scented, which brings luxury to the chore. Mrs. Randolph's back skin is so thin and movable. At first I was afraid to press very hard, but it actually feels good to her when you do. I thought that I would feel embarrassed to do this, but it turns out it's fine. One reason is, they are both so nice, and another reason is, Mr. Randolph acts like it's pure natural.

"So you'll be going to a new school next year, is that right, Katie?" Mr. Randolph asks.

"What?" Mrs. Randolph says. "I didn't hear that, dear."

Mr. Randolph leans in close to Mrs. Randolph's ear and says, "I asked Katie about the school she'll be going to next year."

"Oh, I see."

Mr. Randolph looks at me and smiles and I smile back.

"And what did she say?" asks Mrs. Randolph, and I say, "I didn't say anything yet. But I will be going to a new school, Miller High School."

"Turn me back, will you, Henry? I can't hear her."

Mr. Randolph turns his wife over on her wet back and I tell her louder that I will be starting Miller High School. She nods. *"High school. Well, that's a big step."*

"I guess so," I say.

She leans forward, *"What was that?"*

"Yes," I say.

"You mustn't be afraid, though."

"No."

"What subjects do you like?"

"English."

"Ah, me, too. English was always my favorite."

I smile, nod, then hold up the towel to remind her that we're not quite finished back here.

"Oh, for heaven's sake," she says. "I completely forgot. You'd think we were sitting on a bench and chatting in the park, wouldn't you?" She laughs like she's just heard a good joke.

"It's okay," I say. *"Whenever you're ready."*

Mr. Randolph turns her over again and I wipe her back dry, then put a little powder on her. It's so funny, it's like a baby, but way at the other end of life. Everything is a circle, if you think about it. Mrs. Randolph was doing fine until recently, and then she had a little stroke. She might get some better, but probably not a lot. Mr. Randolph's face when he told me this was full of pain, yet he was smiling.

When we're through bathing Mrs. Randolph, Mr. Randolph says, "I wonder if you could stay with her now while I run out to the grocery store. Would that be all right?"

"Yes, sir," I say. And then, "Do you think she'd like to go outside?"

"Perhaps another time," he says. "It's awfully hot out today, and she doesn't do well in the heat."

"What?" Mrs. Randolph asks, and Mr. Randolph bends over her ear to repeat what he said.

"Oh, I can't tolerate the heat," she says. "Never could. I just wilt. But maybe you could read to me a bit."

"Okay." I wonder if I'll have to yell the whole story. Mr. Randolph hands me a library book by someone called Taylor Caldwell. The title is *The Listener*, which is a very interesting title. Right away you want to know who is this listener, and what is he listening to? Mr. Randolph kisses Mrs. Randolph on the cheek, waves to me, and is gone.

I open to the place that's marked, and start reading. It is someone just talking about their troubles.

"A little louder, dear," Mrs. Randolph says, and there you are, the answer to the yelling part is yes.

I haven't read but two or three pages when I look up and see that Mrs. Randolph is sleeping. And now that I've stopped yelling the story, I can also hear her snoring. It's a ladylike snore, not too loud, just a ruffled kind of breathing. I close the book and put it on my lap, then look at her lying there, her hands folded across her stomach. She wears a blue stone ring, and it is loose on her finger, turned to the side. I think how easy it would be for someone to pluck that ring from her. She is just so vulnerable, like a baby bird in the nest. She also wears a man's watch so that she can see the numbers, and the watch band is twisted and held with a rubber band to be smaller, so it won't fall off. And that is all, except of course for the nightgown. I wonder if she misses her clothes, if she thinks sometimes about how she used to leap out of bed and just get dressed, easy as pie, and now that has gone from her. I can see how some old people get mean and bitter about their lives getting so small, but Mrs. Randolph doesn't seem that way. I think maybe it's because of Mr. Randolph, who takes such good care of her, and even now is buying her the brown bread she wanted because she wants to eat it with some beans for lunch. There is some old people food, for sure. I wonder, Don't they ever just want sloppy joes?

I tiptoe out of the room and go to the hall to use the phone. I have to call Cynthia about the movie tonight, about what time we should meet. When she answers, she sounds mad. "It's me," I say. "What's wrong?"

"Nothing," she says. And waits.

"I'm calling about the movie."

"I'll be there."

"When?" I ask, and she says, "Whenever you say."

"*The Parent Trap* starts at seven," I say. "Want to see that one?" Deep sigh. "Okay."

"What's *wrong*? Did you have a fight with your mother?"

"I can't talk. I'll see you tonight." She hangs up.

I'll bet anything that's what it is; Cynthia is always fighting with her mother, who ought to live in the head room at Bellevue insane asylum. Anyone who says you should always respect your parents would change their minds if they met Mrs. O'Connell.

I go back into the bedroom and sit in the chair and watch Mrs. Randolph sleep. I try to think about what she looked like when she was my age, but I can't imagine it. Even if I saw a picture, the way she is now would still be stubborn in my brain, like she has been that way forever. It seems like you always are the way you are right now, unless you are a movie star, when people always see you the way you were best. Sometimes I wonder, If there is a heaven and people are themselves up there in their bodies, what body is it? The one they died in? It doesn't seem fair if it is, because for one thing, there would be people from car wrecks walking around saying, Well, this isn't how I really looked. But what would be the time that you would say "This is my real look"? My mother always used to say on her birthday that she was twenty-nine, no matter how old she was. So I guess that might be the age.

When I think of my mother now, she is sort of gauzed over, not as clear as she used to be, but still so shining. Her real age when she died was forty-one. It's so funny that I didn't know her age until she died. I look like her around the eyes, and I am so grateful. It is a part of her I will never lose. She had such a nice laugh, like bells. And also she knew how to tap dance a little. One thing I do still remember clearly is that every time she came home from the grocery store with Green Stamps, I was the one who got to put them in the book. We were working on getting the waffle iron. I don't know what ever happened to those books of stamps. I think they got thrown out when we moved, which is a shame; there was at least enough there for a toaster.

I watch Mrs. Randolph's chest rise and fall, listen to the tick of her bedside clock. I practice different ways of crossing my legs, while in my head I conjugate the French verb *être*. One thing I hope they don't do in high school is ask you to write about what you did on your summer vacation and then read it aloud. I would be Sominex to the entire class.

WELL, I MIGHT AS WELL GO SHOPPING for a crystal ball and a silk scarf to wrap around my head, because once again I have told the future. Cynthia and I are sitting around her bedroom late on this Friday night after having watched the kids in front of us kiss so much it would be a wonder if they saw anything that happened on the screen. Forget the movie; this was the real show: The boy and girl come in together, a little ways apart. The boy has on a clean shirt and is wearing a belt on his pants and you can see the comb marks in his hair. The girl has a necklace on with her dress and nylon stockings, and her hair got washed that afternoon—she has the aura of Prell. Lights dim, and three seconds later, kiss, kiss, kiss. Next, slouch way down in the seat, and then the boy does something that the girl starts giggling and says, "*Stop!*" You would think they would have the decency to sit in the back, but no, they must put themselves smack in the middle of the theater so all can see. Cynthia and I sat there with popcorn boxes on our lap, and I felt like we were in kindergarten making macaroni necklaces.

Now, just as we are making ourselves comfortable, we have the horror of her mother sticking her head in. "Everything fine up here?" she asks, and her eyeballs seem like they're sticking out three miles. I look around for broken bones and other catastrophes and then say, Yes, everything is fine.

36

"Cynthia?" Mrs. O'Connell asks, and Cynthia sighs. "*Yes,* Mother, everything is *fine.*"

"A little girl talk, huh?" Mrs. O'Connell says.

Neither of us says anything, and finally she closes the door.

Cynthia turns the radio up loud, so no one can hear us. It's Fab Freddy, talking about a rocking Friday night on 99.9 FM. I wish I could be doing the show with him. "And now, a record that my good friend Katie picked," he could say. "All you lovebirds cuddle up, here comes Bobby *Vinton.*"

"I hate my mother so much," Cynthia says, and I say, "Me, too," to give support, even though I don't hate her; I just think she's pathetic.

"You know when you called and I was in a bad mood?"

"Yeah," I say. I kind of want to ask *which* time, but that would only put her in a worse mood. It used to be that Cynthia was only goofy, but now she is moody.

"Well, it's because of something my mother is doing."

"What's she doing?" I love when you ask a question and you know that no matter what the answer is, it will be delicious.

She lies back on the floor, her autograph hound serving as her pillow. So far I am the only one to sign it. "Write big!" Cynthia said, and I did, but now I regret it, because every time I come in her room, there it is "Best wishes, Luff, Katie Nash!!!!" and that is all that's on the dog, and the writing is not even good.

Cynthia sighs. "I don't know if I can say it. It's so embarrassing."

Now I am on full alert like the dogs at the dinner table. "Tell me," I say, and turn the radio up even louder.

"She is going to become a Girl Scout leader," Cynthia says, "and I have to be in her troop." She looks up at me quickly, then away.

"Oh, no."

"Yes."

And I thought I was doomed for having to baby-sit for a summer job. "When?"

"The first meeting is next week. Here."

Cynthia opens her closet and digs around in the back, then pulls out a green dress and holds it out, which at first I don't get, and then I realize it's a Girl Scout uniform. "She's going to sew patches on it," Cynthia says, "and then I have to wear it. And that's not all." She goes to the closet again, and pulls out a beret.

"Oh, Cynthia," I say. "We have to talk to her."

"I did."

"Why is she doing this?"

"So we can be *closer*." Cynthia puts the dress and the beret back in the closet, shuts the door, and lies back down on the floor. Little tears are sprouting out of her eyes, and she brushes them away like she would like to murder them.

"But you're too old," I say.

"She doesn't think so."

"I'll help you. We'll think of something."

Cynthia sits up. Already she feels better. All it takes sometimes is to know you are not alone.

"Maybe we could . . . ," I say, but then I fizzle out.

"I don't know if this would work, but we could—"

"Hold on!" I say, my hand held up in the air. "Listen!"

"Okay, you jet-setters," Fab Freddy is saying. "Listen up now, because what you just heard is true. We've selected a winner for our travel contest!"

I want to hear who wins the contest that I also entered, and whether they spaz out on the phone like winners usually do, start screaming and say I don't *believe* it, I don't *believe* it. But right now a miracle has happened here in Cynthia's bedroom, because I hear these words: "The winner is . . . *Katie Nash*. All right!

Congratulations, Katie! You've got ninety-nine minutes to call in and claim your prize, baaaaaby!"

"Oh, my God," I say, my hand over my mouth. I am freezing and boiling.

Cynthia's eyes are wide. "Does he mean *you?*" she asks. "Is it *you?*"

I nod, and then get the terrible feeling that there is another Katie Nash, who is probably seventeen and saying, "Cool! I won!"

"It might be me," I say, but now doubt is crowding in so bad, my mind is saying, "Now, wait a minute. *Did* you enter that contest?"

And it's stereo, because Cynthia is saying, "Did you enter that contest?"

I nod, afraid to speak.

"Well, then, call!" Cynthia says, and hands me her princess phone.

"But what if two Katie Nashes entered?" I ask. "What if it's another one?"

"It's not!"

"But it could be!"

"But you have to find *out!*"

I start to dial, then say, "But wait . . . do you have to wait until ninety-nine minutes?"

"*No!* You have ninety-nine minutes to call before it's *too late!*" Cynthia picks up the receiver. "*I'm* calling."

"Okay," I say. "But if it's me, I'll talk."

"Oh, what's the number, what's the number, I forgot!" Cynthia says, and for a minute I almost don't know either, even though I hear that number every night. But then I remember and I tell her, and she dials. Then she starts laughing, wheezy excited, looking at me with her eyes all wide, and she has to turn her back on me so she can get serious again.

I sit with one hand squeezing the other to death and hear her say. "Yes, I'm calling about the travel contest? You just announced the winner?" Then there is a pause of about three hundred years. She turns to look at me, all lit up, and then says, "No, I'm not Katie Nash, but she's right here." She is nodding her head up and down real fast. "Yes," she says, and then "All right, I will." She turns down the radio, then hands the phone to me, and all of a sudden it seems like everything in the universe has stopped dead in its tracks. "Hello?" I say.

"Katie?" a woman's voice says.

"Yes, ma'am."

"Hi! I'd like to verify that you're Katie Nash of 1617 Melrose Drive, St. Louis. Is that right?"

"Yes," I say, in a mouse voice.

"Well, congratulations! Now, hold on for a second for Freddy, and remember to keep your radio down, okay?"

"Okay."

"We'll have you on the air in just a minute."

Oh my God, my insides are saying, but I can't give in. One minute, kid, the next minute, famous. I knew something big would happen this summer, I knew it. I sit straight up and look only at Cynthia's walls because if I look at her, forget it.

I hear Freddy doing a commercial in the background plus on the radio, but he is ahead of himself on the phone. I wonder if something is wrong. But then, "Hi, there, Katie!" Fab Freddy says. It's him, I know his voice, it is the real Fab Freddy on the telephone with me.

"Hello," I say back and feel like smacking myself on the head for how I sound. Then, "Hi," I say, like he did—all casual and friendly.

"Congratulations!" he says. "You're our winner!"

"Yes," I say, "thank you."

"Are you excited?"

"Yes, sir." Then, "Wow!" I add.

"So! Where in the world are we sending you, Katie Nash?"

"Oh! . . . Um, to Texas?"

"*Texas*, Welllllll, where at in Texas? San Antonio, I'll bet! Suck down some of those margaritas, down by that ol' green river!" Then he makes a bunch of high Mexican sounds, with lots of yips and rolling Rs. "Is that where you're headed, darlin'?"

"No, sir. I'm going to Ford Hood."

"To what?"

"Fort Hood?"

"Fort *Hood!* And where is that, Katie?"

"It's in Killeen."

"Ah ha! . . . And where is Killeen?" He says *Killeen* like he's saying *Xmqtriwzxm.*

"Well, kind of in the heart. In the heart of Texas."

"*The stars are bright,*" Freddy sings.

"Yes, sir."

"Well now, what in the world made you pick *Fort Hood,* Katie?"

Now the air hangs so heavy and I realize I could have said New York City. Or Paris, France! But I say, "I used to live there, and I want to see a friend."

"Okay!" Freddy says. "Well, you're on your way, kiddo! Have a great time, and what radio station is the best in the world?"

Well, I have no idea.

"Katie?" Freddy says.

"Yes, sir?"

"What radio station is the best in the world?"

"*KOOL!*" Cynthia is whispering. "*KOOL!*"

Oh.

"*KOOL,*" I say.

"You got it!" Freddy says. "And now, in your honor, let's listen to *Travelin' Man!*"

And he is gone. The woman comes back on the phone to tell me she'll be sending me an airplane ticket as soon as she gets my parents' permission—they'll need to call her at the station. I say okay and hang up the phone.

41

And then I just sit there. I want to replay everything that just happened and never forget it.

"You won!" Cynthia says. "Wow! I didn't even know you entered!"

"I know," I say. "I didn't tell you. I didn't tell anyone."

"Uh-oh," Cynthia says. And I know what she means. I see myself saying, "Hey, Dad, I won a free trip to Texas!" And him, a fork on the way to his mouth, stopped in midair, What did you say? His prelude to no.

SATURDAY NIGHT AND I AM at the kitchen table with the Wexler boys, who are finally being quiet because I told them I can do card tricks. Really, I only know two, but so far it is enough to keep them happy. Each one wants to have it done to him only, and the others can't watch—they have to sit there with their eyes shut. Fine with me. A sip of RC cola, a dip into the chips, and do the trick again—that is my job for the rest of the evening. In half an hour, they have to go to bed. I don't care whether they sleep on not; my duties are done once they are sent to bed. I can watch TV and read Mrs. Wexler's magazines, even though they are not really for me; they are mainly about how to cook chicken in marinade or gardening. Sometimes there is a short story that's good, like about a reporter who thinks she will never fall in love, but does.

Mr. and Mrs. Wexler went out to a movie and he seemed all happy about it, and she seemed like they were going to work on a chain gang. I like Mr. Wexler so much. He's always in a good mood and he always gives me an extra dollar when he pays me. He has the bluest eyes. He goes bowling every week, and he has his own bag and a bowling shirt with *Buddy* written on it in turquoise blue embroidery. There's a picture on the shirt of two bowling pins getting knocked sky high, and the bowling ball is winking.

"How did you *do* that?" Mark asks, about my four kings trick, and I shrug and say, "It's magic."

And now they have to shuffle around because once again it's David's turn, and he has announced that this time, he's going to figure out how I do it. One thing about magic, if you know how to do it, people like you, at least while you're doing the trick. But naturally David doesn't figure it out, and then it's Henry's turn, while David and Mark play smash the chip into a thousand pieces and then suck it up off the table like a vacuum cleaner. Mrs. Wexler buys cheap potato chips called by the store's name, which is always the giveaway. I wish she would get Lays or Ripple Chips plus some Dr Pepper. But she has not asked me for my opinion.

"I'll bet you don't know *one* thing, though," Henry says, after David has once again not figured out the trick and now is pretend-banging his head on the table.

"What's that?" I say, eating another crummy chip. She could at least get barbecue.

Henry straightens in his seat. "Okay. What is the last number?"

"The last number of what?" I say.

"The last number in the world."

I stare at him, and David puts his head in his hands like his dog died and says, "Oh, no, Henry, not that again."

Henry pays no attention to his brother. He stares at me, and says, "Any number you say, I just add one, and it never *stops*." He looks a little sad.

"Well, infinity," I say.

"What?"

"Infinity." I say again. "That's what you say when you mean it goes on and on, there is no end."

He stares at me. His glasses are so thick.

"There's a symbol for it," I say. "Give me a pencil and I'll show you."

All three boys rush for one of the kitchen drawers. Everything is a contest. I forgot you have to say for one of them to do things or they fight over it. Amazingly, Henry wins, and he hands me the pencil and I draw the symbol on a napkin.

They all crowd around like it's the baby with three heads.

"That's it?" Mark asks, and David says, "Dope, that's an eight!"

"It is not," I say.

"It is so, just an eight lying down!"

"But that's it. That's the symbol for infinity."

They all look at me, and I say, once again, "It is! You can look it up!"

"I wouldn't make that the symbol if I were them," Henry says. "It is just an eight lying down."

I look at my watch. "All right. You have ten minutes before bed. Each of you, make a new symbol for infinity."

And I am baby-sitter of the year, because don't they hop to it. David makes an arrow with curlicues on it. Mark makes a circle in a circle in a circle, which I must admit is pretty good. And Henry makes an asterisk. "That is already a symbol," I tell him, "and it does not stand for infinity."

He looks up at me and I see a blue vein running up his neck that reminds me that he is a human being and it is a miracle how blood keeps us alive and how all our organs are always working without us paying any attention. "It is already a symbol," I say again. I am sorry to disappoint him, but I think he should know.

"A symbol for what?" he asks.

"It's an asterisk," I say, "and—" Henry starts laughing.

"What's so funny?" I ask, and he says, "Asterisk. It's a dirty word."

He acts like this is pure hysterical, but I know it's because he's tired; when kids get tired they can start acting like nothing at all is the funniest thing in the world.

"It is not dirty," I say, "it is an asterisk, and it signifies 'something missing.' "

"Not tonight," Henry says. "Tonight it means the last number."

45

"Okay," I say, and look at my watch again. Hallelujah, I have made it. It is time for them to go to sleep and me to take off my shoes and rest my feet on the coffee table while I decide: magazine or television. If I lived in my own house, it would be luxury time like that all the time. Magazine, I might decide, and then I would go and get some *good* potato chips to eat while I read it.

I tuck them all in, David and Mark in the bunk beds in one room, which smells like socks, and Henry in his bed in the real little room that he has alone that smells like apples, I don't know why. Model airplanes hang from his ceiling, and he has an old brown bear with no eyes that he sleeps with but he won't pick it up in front of me. I like to tuck Henry in, because he isn't embarrassed; he likes when I pull the sheet up under his chin. Tonight he gets the bonus that I sit on the bed beside him like a real mother. "Good night," I say, and he rubs his eyes and yawns and it makes for this little hurt of pleasure inside me like when you see baby kittens sitting there blinking in the sun, they just have no idea.

SUNDAY NIGHT, WE ARE EATING DINNER, when I all of a sudden take in a deep breath and bring it up. "Dad? I entered this contest on the radio, and guess what, I won!"

"You won what?" he says, and then gestures with his chin toward the bread, which means Ginger should pass it to him.

"I won a trip."

He stops buttering his bread. "To where?"

"To Texas. On an airplane. Well, I could have gone anywhere I wanted, but I picked Fort Hood. Now I can go back and visit Cherylanne!"

He looks at Ginger, whose blank and innocent face is like her shrugging her shoulders and saying, Don't ask me.

"You're not going on any trip," he says.

I look at Ginger, who is looking into her plate. *Not my business*. He is not angry, but he could get that way if I push.

But I have to. Very quietly, I say, "Why not?"

He looks up and I sit still.

"You don't need to be taking a trip that far away by yourself." Forkful of meat loaf, chew, chew. Shakes his head. "No."

"Would this all have been free?" Ginger asks. It's like under the table, we are holding hands.

"What did I *say*?" he yells, and that's it, game over, no winner.

"May I be excused?" I say, and I don't wait for an answer before

I go to my room and close the door. I sit at the edge of my bed and start crying. I should have known that he would never go for this. Cynthia knew, and she's not even his daughter. I hold a pillow to my middle, rock back and forth. What if this is the only time I ever win anything, and now I can't even go. I think of how I would have been high in the sky looking out the little round window. How I would have come to Cherylanne's house like a celebrity. How we would have gone to her room like old times and talked and gone to the swimming pool again. And then I stop thinking about it, because this dream has been ground out like one of his cigarettes in his beanbag ashtray. I don't think it's right for a parent to have so much control over another person's whole life, even if they are a kid. Some things you could at least talk about. Other families do that. On *Father Knows Best,* he would let Princess go. Probably not Kitten, but I am much older than she is. Now I will have to call Fab Freddy and say I can't go: *Hello, this is Katie Nash, and I am still a baby who can't do anything. Just give the prize to someone else, thank you.*

I start to look at a *Seventeen* that I've already read three hundred times when I hear him calling me. I crack open my door, yell, "Yes, sir?"

"Dishes," he says.

You would think when you have had your dream smashed you at least could forget about dishes. But no. I start down the hall and I hear Ginger say, "Never mind, Katie, I'll do them."

I hear the deep voice of my father start to say something, and then the fast, light words of Ginger. She will take care of him; I am free. I go back to my bedroom and close my door again and get the faint hope that maybe she can talk him into letting me go. I think of Diane, wonder what she's doing right this minute out there in California. It is five o'clock. Maybe she is on the bus, on her way home from the office where she is a typist, and men are looking at her; they always look at her, because she's so beautiful. If they are, I know what she might do. Sometimes when some guy was staring at her, she would say, "Take a picture, it lasts longer." Another thing she used to say is, "Take a good look while you've got a chance; prices go up tomorrow." Men would laugh then, but it was an unsure laugh, and in their eyes would be some hatred.

It is such a strange and dark secret that Diane is hardly ever in touch with us. We have only been to see her once, my father and I, and we all slept in the living room because she has what they call a studio apartment. She had so few dishes in the cupboard, two or three plates, two glasses, only one cup. A set of silverware for four, so thin and light it bent in your hand if you pressed down too hard. Weeds grew out in the front yard of the corner apartment building where she lives, but, it being California, they were pretty weeds. We didn't do much there—took a walk around the city of Sacramento, went out to a little restaurant where nobody talked much, we just ate some Mexican food, cheese enchiladas. When we left, my father tried to give Diane some money, but she wouldn't take it. "I don't need it, I'm fine," she kept saying, but then at the end, she did take it. My father tried to hug her good-bye, which he learned from Ginger, but Diane only stiffened like he was hurting her. I guess he was.

Diane is like a sword in my father's side, Ginger told me. Maybe that could help in getting him to change his mind about my trip. I might go out and just mention Diane. I stand up, thinking of what I might say, then sit back down. I don't need to mention her if she is a sword in his side. He feels it all the time. And yet, look.

A T NINE O'CLOCK, I call Cynthia and tell her the grim news. "Oh, I knew it," she says. "I knew he wouldn't let you go."

I say nothing, stare at the little round paper circle on the phone that tells the number, TWinbrook 3-6409. I wonder who gets to make up the names for telephone numbers. Here would be mine: UNfair 3-6409.

"Did you call the radio station?" Cynthia asks.

"No."

"You have to call them, so they can give it to someone else."

"I know that, Cynthia." I fill up my cheeks with air, then blow it all out.

"I'm sorry," she says. "I would help you if I could. You want me to call him? Or my mom? Want her to call him?"

"Your mom!"

"Yeah. She could say she would let me go, if I won."

"She wouldn't let you go! She hardly lets you go out without a sweater when it's five hundred degrees outside!"

"I know. But one thing she likes is travel. She thinks it's 'broadening.' She actually might let me go. You want me to ask her to call your father?"

I think about this for a minute, imagine Mrs. O'Connell calling him. But then, "No thanks," I say. "It would only make him mad."

"I can tell you something that is even worse than you can't go to Texas," Cynthia says.

"What?"

"My mother is planning a camping experience for her Girl Scout troop."

"When?"

"In three weeks."

"Do you have to go?"

"Of course. But here's the queer part: It's going to be *inside!* It's going to be in our living room!"

"What?"

"Yes! Because my mother doesn't like the woods because it's all dirty there."

I can just see Mrs. O'Connell out in the middle of the woods, beautiful bird sounds all around, the sun shining through the trees like rays from heaven, and her with her cleaning kerchief on, sweeping violently and spraying Country Fresh deodorizer all over the place. But how in the world do you pitch a tent in the middle of a living room?

"You can't go camping inside!" I say.

"That's what I said. And she said she is the leader and what she says, goes. She says we will sleep in sleeping bags and make our hobo dinners in tinfoil packets and cook them in the fireplace, and we'll tell ghost stories and have s'mores and look at some books on nature, so what's the difference? Plus we have to make 'eyes of god' with Popsicle sticks and yarn."

"Oh, man."

"I know."

"We are both of us losers," I say. It just slips out, and even though I'm sorry to say it, it kind of makes me feel better.

"We are not," Cynthia says.

Right.

I AM IN THAT PLACE JUST BEFORE SLEEP where even though things are real they could also be a dream. I see my door open and in comes my father. It's real: I smell Old Spice. I sit up.

"You awake?" he says.

"Yes, sir." *And don't think I'm not still mad at you, because I am still mad at you.*

He pulls out my desk chair and turns on my desk light.

I hold my hands up over my eyes, and he moves the lamp so it's behind his back and not so bright.

"I have changed my mind about your going to Texas," he says.

I don't move one muscle.

"All right?"

I nod. "Yes, sir." Very, very quietly, I clear my throat.

"You go ahead and go back to sleep; tomorrow we'll make all the arrangements. You can stay for two days, and two days only."

"Okay."

"All right?"

"Yes, sir."

"All right."

He snaps off the light, comes over to stand beside me. He is so tall. "Good night," he says.

He goes out the door and closes the door behind him. I squeeze my pillow really tight, but that is not enough so I happy-punch it a few times. I think of myself getting on the airplane and waving good-bye and I have to leap up and do the quietest happiness dance, just a few steps like the Pony, and inside me there is an open mouth shouting *yahoo!* Then I lie back down, but I am way too excited to sleep. I get up and go to my desk and start my list of things to bring. "Present for Belle" is the first thing I write, because she is the main hostess. Hankies or bubble bath. I know why I can only stay two days. Benjamin Franklin said, "Fish and visitors smell in three days." We had that in junior high English. I was having a bad day that day because when the teacher called on me to explain what it meant, I thought it meant they didn't wash. Although I didn't say that. I just said, "Well, I think it's sort of self-explanatory." But then another girl raised her hand and said, all smug, "*Don't* overstay your *wel*come." The idea is you might be really happy to see someone, but then they get on your nerves because you're sick of them and you just want your normal life back. But if they leave before three days, you might even kind of miss them.

"Underwear," I write next, which is pretty obvious, but you might as well write it down because what if you did forget. There you would be the next day, staring at your open suitcase and thinking, Uh oh. "Bathing suit," I write. "Nice dress for going out," because we might. I start thinking of going out with Cherylanne and a funny thing happens: I think of Cynthia instead. How I will miss her. How I might send her a postcard.

I guess it has become home here, now. There are reasons for coming back. I have the responsibility of my jobs, and there is the interesting dilemma of how to save Cynthia from a mother gone berserk. It's so amazing how that happens, place after place. When your dad is in the army, it's like you're always saying, "Okay, this is home." And then, "No. *This* is home." And so on and so on forever. But the joke is that you are never home except inside yourself. That is where you have to make the place with the light always on, a chair always waiting, *sit down*. It is always the same light, and it is always the same chair, turned just so and never moving one inch.

M ONDAY EVENING AFTER DINNER, I am allowed to call Cherylanne. My father has spoken with the radio station, and TWA will send me tickets for whenever I want. The kitchen timer is set for Cherylanne and me to talk three minutes; then my father will take over and talk to Belle. I go into the hall and dial her number, then slide down onto the floor, my back against the wall, get ready. The phone rings and right away a boy answers. "Bubba?" I say. I can feel my heart beating so fast in my chest.

A pause. A burp. Then, "Yeah?"

Well, Bubba has not changed. "This is Katie!"

Nothing.

"I used to live next door to you?"

Nothing.

"Hello?" I say.

"Oh *yeah*," he says, his voice lazy like he just woke up. "I remember you. You had that sister, Diane, she was *always* getting in trouble. And y'all got a puppy just before y'all left."

I really do not need for Bubba to tell me my life history, since I am more aware than he is of how the story goes.

"How you doing?" he asks.

Well, here I have the problem that I don't want to be rude, but I don't want to use my three minutes talking to Bubba. It turns out

54

that I don't have to say a thing, though, because in the background I hear Cherylanne's familiar voice saying, "Is that Katie *Nash?*" And there is her voice in my ear, saying, "Katie? Is that you?"

"Yes," I say, and I am smiling so hard I can hardly talk. "I'm calling to say I'm coming to visit you, if it's okay! For two days. On an airplane!"

"You are?"

"Yes, if it's okay. I won a trip from a radio contest. I could pick anywhere, and I picked to come and see you!"

A moment, and then, "You could have gone *anywhere?*"

"Yes."

"Wow. I would have picked Hollywood."

"Well," I say.

"But I'm glad you're coming! When?"

"I can come almost anytime."

"Mom!" Cherylanne calls. "Katie's coming to visit! Can she come next weekend?"

Another pause, and then Belle is on the phone. "Well, sweet-heart, how *are* you?"

"Fine, thank you," I say, and I see my three minutes going down the drain.

"We would be *delighted* to have you; when are you coming?"

"My dad will talk to you about that," I say. "I was just going to talk to Cherylanne first. I have three minutes, and then my dad will talk to you."

"Oh!" she says. "Well, let me put her back on."

And there Cherylanne is again, her breathy "Hi!"

"Hi," I say, and all of a sudden I am shy. My hand goes into a fist, like it always does when I feel like this.

"Did you get my letter about Darren?" Her voice is low and a bit muffled, as though she has her hand over the phone.

"Yes." Now I relax a bit and lower my voice too. I love this. Me and another person, boxed off from the world.

"Believe me, I have plenty more to tell you. And now you can meet him, too! I *never* thought that would happen. I swear, it just goes to show you."

"Yes."

"We can do a lot of things," Cherylanne says. "What do you want to do first?"

I think about this. We are not exactly the same as we used to be.

"Katie?"

"Yeah?"

"Don't worry. It will all be delirious surprises, okay?"

And *ding!* Our talk time is over. I say good-bye to Cherylanne and hand the phone to my father. "Flight arrangements," he is saying. "Arrival." "Departure." About me. Queen of Sheba. Flying through the sky on my own visit to my own friend because of something I did, by myself.

IN THE MORNING, I head over to Cynthia's house. I have a few hours before I have to go to the Randolphs', and Cynthia had an excellent idea. I used my baby-sitting money on a bottle of QT and we are both going to use it and then enjoy the miracle of tanning in her bedroom while we plan how to get her out of Girl Scouts. Cynthia's mother needs to understand that when you're a teenager you make your own kind of Girl Scout troop, because you and your friends do the stuff you care about automatically. You don't need somebody's mom making you do things on a checklist to earn a badge that you sew on a sash and then go around wearing like an idiot.

When I get to Cynthia's house, I see her leaning out her bedroom window, waving me over. "Come here!" she whispers urgently, and looks all around to see if anyone is watching. I point to the door, and she hisses, "No! Come over *here!*"

I go to her window and she says, "Climb in."

I stare at her. "Why?"

"I need to know if it can be done."

"Well, why don't you try it, then?" I stand back so she can jump out. It actually looks pretty easy to get back in; the window is fairly low to the ground.

"I *can't* do it," she says. "If somebody sees, I could get in trouble."

"Why won't I get in trouble?"

"Because," Cynthia says, "it's not your house. It's not your *mother*. Just do it, okay? See if you can."

I don't understand this, but I hoist myself up on the windowsill, then slide in to her room. It scrapes my stomach a bit, but it's not that hard. "Ta da," I say.

"Oh, good," she says. "Now I know I have an escape route."

"From what?"

"I don't know. The camp-out, for one thing."

It's a good thing I'm here. Cynthia has become desperate. "You won't have to do that," I say. "We'll both talk to her, one at a time, and then together."

She sighs. "You don't know my mother."

"Yes, I do," I say, grimly. In my mind is the fixed smile of Mrs. O'Connell. "Don't worry, we'll think of something. But first . . ." I hold up the bag from the drugstore, pull out the QT.

"You got it!" She gives me a sly, sideways look. "Guess what I thought of?"

"What?"

"We could be tan *all over.*"

Although Cynthia has become my good friend, my only one here, really, I am not too comfortable about the idea of being bare naked with her. Plus, if her mother saw *that,* she'd drop dead. "I think I just want to do bathing suits," I say.

Cynthia shrugs. "Okay."

I take off my shorts and shirt to reveal my bathing suit. It's black-and-white checked and has daisies on it.

"Is that new?" Cynthia asks, and I tell her it is; I got it from Ginger for my trip.

"I have a new one, too," Cynthia says. "Wait till you see. I'll go put it on. Don't start till I get back."

I sit down on the floor to wait, even though I'm dying to get going. In only three hours, I will have a beautiful tan—I'm going to double-dose myself.

When Cynthia comes back in, she is wearing a black bikini. I can't believe it. The last suit I saw her in was pink-and-white polka dots and it had a little skirt. "Where'd you get *that?*"

"I sent away for it in a magazine. With the money my grandmother sent me for my birthday."

I swallow, try to think of something to say. I remember something I saw in one of Mrs. Wexler's magazines: "Be Boston in public and French in private." This is pretty French.

"Do you like it?" Cynthia asks, and the shadow of doubt is upon her.

"I love it!" I say, and she smiles. Then I ask, "Did your mother see it?"

Cynthia looks at me and her face is a billboard of the answer *no!* "I hid it in a shoebox in a closet in the basement," she says. "This is the first time I've worn it." She stands on her tiptoes to see as much of herself as she can in her dresser mirror. Her belly button goes out, but mine goes in. She slides her shoulder straps down and says, "If you do my back, I'll do yours."

I look at the clock. At one, we'll be done.

A T TWO O'CLOCK, I ring the bell at the Randolphs'. Mr. Randolph opens it right away and his smile drops off his face. "Oh, my."

"I know," I say.

"What happened?"

"QT." I wish he would let me in.

"What's that?"

"It's supposed to be a quick tan, from a bottle. But . . ." I look down at my orange self. I could throw up.

"Ah," he says. "Well, it will fade. Surely it will fade."

"I guess," I say. And then, "Do you think you should tell your wife before I go in there so she isn't too shocked?" I see her clutching her chest, her eyes bugging out, *"Henry?????"*

"I think she'll be just fine," he says, and he's right. When we walk into Mrs. Randolph's room, she's sitting up in the wheelchair beside her bed. When she sees me, at first she holds really still, and we just stare at each other. In my head, there's a little voice counting, "One . . . two . . ." And then Mrs. Randolph slaps her knee and starts laughing so hard nothing comes out but wheezing. And I start laughing too. And I know at this moment that Cynthia isn't my only friend.

"QT?" she asks.

I nod. "I used a little too much."

"I've seen the ads for it," she said. "I *thought* that's what would happen!"

"Well, I wish you'd told me first," I say.

"What's that?" she says, and I repeat myself louder.

"It won't last," she says, kind. And then we laugh out the last little bit of our dismay.

THIS IS THE KIND OF SUNSET that makes you believe in God. I'm sitting out in the backyard looking at a sky so full of pale pink and lavender I feel like crying. I have Bones, the big skinny mutt, on one side of me and Bridgett, the almost-cocker spaniel, on the other, and even they seem affected, lying so quietly with serious looks on their dog faces.

I wonder sometimes if dogs think about humans, about how we act. I wonder if they see us getting dressed and think, Hmmm, now why in the world are they doing that? I wonder if they see us get into cars and think, Why don't they just run there? I'll bet they think we're crazy for not spending a lot more time outdoors.

I'm out here to try to cool off after taking a boiling hot shower. My father's idea. When he saw my QT glow, he didn't know what to do. Ginger, laughing, told him that it happened all the time, that she in fact had once turned herself orange, and that seemed to help him from getting mad. He pulled me over to the sink and rubbed my arm with some dish soap and water: nothing. Then cleanser. Nothing. Then he told me to go take a long, hot shower. And that did seem to help some, but basically I guess time will have to do the trick. I wish I could arrest whoever made QT. It is a pure lie. But all I can do is write a letter to the company to at least try to get my money back; that was Ginger's idea. She said she wished she had thought of it when it happened to her. I said I could ask for two-for-one, but she said never mind, she would just cosign my letter about myself.

I lie back and Bridgett rests her nose on my stomach, like she feels sorry for me. Say what you want about dogs, I think they're smarter than humans. You don't see them walking around turned orange from trying to be tan. If they did get tan, they wouldn't think it was a big deal anyway; they'd just be interested to know when the next meal was coming or the next rabbit running by. Bones caught a rabbit once and killed him. I hate those things where it's just nature but it hurts your feelings so bad. A lot of things in life are like that. In fact, you could say life is like that.

I take in a huge breath and look at the sky as hard as I can. I feel like I'm trying to eat it with my eyes. I wish there would be certain things you come across and you could say, Okay, that's one. Put that away for me to pull out later just exactly as it is now. My dream is for me to be a poet who could make things like this sky come to life for someone else. If you see a sunset and try and describe it to someone in normal words, all you can say is, "Boy, I saw a great sunset last night." But if you are a poet, you give it to someone to feel for themselves. Like you make a little seed of what you saw, they swallow it, and it blooms again inside their own heart.

I see the shadow of my father at the screen door. I know he'll stand there for a minute, and then turn on the yellow porch light and call me in. I wish I could stay out longer. The air is so soft and warm, the fireflies are coming, and time has that slowed down feeling. If a summer were a girl, she'd always be lying stretched out in the grass in a long white dress, her arms over her head, her eyes half closed.

Now the sky is dark, and the stars come out, arranged in their ancient patterns. There is the belt of Orion. The Big Dipper. The North Star. What a name that is, *North Star*. It's as satisfying to say as a good dinner is to eat.

The porch light goes on. Every time I feel like this and have to come in, I lie in bed and feel the earth whisper my name, like it's trying to tell me I forgot something out there, and to come back and get it. But I won't ask to stay out longer. It could start an argument, and the sound of angry words at this moment would be like desecrating a church. I get up and head inside. I wish I could leave a trail of gratefulness behind me that you could see, glowing thanks. I would pay to see stars, but I never have to. This to me is one of those miracles.

So, MRS. O'CONNELL," I say. I clear my throat. "First, I want to thank you for letting me talk to you in private." We are sitting at the kitchen table, and my hands are folded and resting exactly in front of me, which is the way world leaders do it when they have peace talks. Except for Mr. Khrushchev, who is fond of using his shoe to bang on the table. "I really appreciate it," I say. Cynthia is waiting in her bedroom, probably biting her nails to the quick.

"That's quite all right," Mrs. O'Connell says, and she's so stiff her lips hardly move at all when she says this. She tries a little smile that gets an F.

"This is about the Girl Scout troop idea," I say, and Mrs. O'Connell says, "I'm well aware of that." She stirs her coffee with her fancy little spoon from Belgium. She has a whole wooden rack of spoons from different countries hung up on the wall of the kitchen. Each day she uses a different one for her coffee. She's wearing a lime green shift, and has a filmy yellow scarf tied in her hair. If you didn't know her, you'd see her and think, *What a pretty woman*. But after you talked to her about five minutes, you would only think, *Eeeeeeyikes!* Ordinarily I would be nervous about talking to her about anything; I mostly just like to avoid her. But I feel so bad for Cynthia. And I don't know why, but the fact that I'm going to Texas in three days makes me feel strong.

"I have talked a lot with Cynthia about it," I say, "and she so much appreciates your asking her and everything like that, but we were wondering if maybe she isn't a little old to be doing this."

"Too old to be doing what?"

I stare at her for a moment, then shrug. "Well . . . like . . . camping out." Then, in a smaller voice, "In the living room."

"Well," she laughs. "I hardly think she's too old to be camping out. Many adults camp out. In fact, you have to be old enough *to* camp out; there are many dangerous things you have to learn to do. For example, do you know how to start a fire, Katie?"

"No, ma'am," I say, and in the back of my brain is: "It's not something that comes up for me to have to do too often. These days, we have stoves and heat built right in."

"Would you know what to prepare to eat in the woods?"

"No, ma'am." Ditto the same kind of thing in the back of my brain, having to do with grocery stores and kitchens.

"What about protection from wildlife?"

"Well," I say, "excuse me, but I don't think there's going to be too much wildlife in your living room."

"That is hardly the point," she says. If she were a cartoon lady, icicles would be hanging from her word bubble. "If you were in the real woods, you might not run across any wildlife, either. But you should be prepared. It is a skill that can serve you all your life, to know how to survive in the woods. You never know, Katie. You just never know."

I sigh. "Mrs. O'Connell, the thing is, it's kind of embarrassing to be a Girl Scout when you're a teenager. Like maybe in the old days it was good, but now it's kind of embarrassing."

She sits up straighter and I see the flash of hurt in her eyes. Her mouth tightens a notch more.

"I mean, it's a really good idea for you to do it for the ones that want to. But Cynthia is the kind of kid that Girl Scouts is not a good idea for. And me, too, no offense against the Girl Scouts, but we are just not the right type."

"Uh huh. And I wonder why it is that Cynthia hasn't told me this."

"She tried."

"Oh, no, she didn't. Uh-uh. She certainly did not."

I know what she thinks. She thinks I, Katie Nash, juvenile delinquent, have corrupted her daughter, who was so excited about wearing her dumb green beret and holding up fingers to say the Girl Scout pledge, until I had to go and ruin it. I shift a bit on my chair, and then say, "Yes, ma'am, she *did* try to tell you, but you aren't too good a listener."

Silence like a roar.

And now I might as well go all the way, because I'm probably going to get kicked out of here and will have to see Cynthia on the sly, like Romeo and Juliet, only two girls. "You are hard to talk to; you mostly are always just telling her what to do. And you treat her like she doesn't know how to take care of herself, but she does. Like she knows when she's cold and when she has had enough to eat; she isn't a baby. Plus, you shouldn't expect that she should always have to tell you everything, because we are teens now, and some things should be private." I am not even looking at her. I am looking my hands and just talking away, and I am saying everything to Mrs. O'Connell about Cynthia, but I am also saying everything about myself to my own parents. "Kids need to have some respect too. Like you don't let her put any pictures from magazines up on her walls, and even my dad lets me do that, and he's really strict."

I hear loud breathing coming from Mrs. O'Connell. Here it comes. She will say something about would I like to escort myself out or should she help me find the door. But when I look up, I see her staring into her coffee cup and there are two tears perched on the edge of her lids.

I swallow, then look around the kitchen for help. Like Dear Abby will pop out of the walls and sit down at the table and say,

"Well, now, let's just wake up and smell the coffee." But it is just us two, and I have said too much. "Mrs. O'Connell?"

She waves her hand, *no*.

"Um . . . I'm sorry if I hurt your feelings."

"Oh, I know you're only trying to help," Mrs. O'Connell says. "I know she hates me. She's my only child and she . . ." She sniffles, holds back a sob. "I know she hates me. I thought this would . . . I'm only trying . . ." And now tears really do come gushing out of this grown woman. "I never had good mothering myself," she says. "And I wanted so much, when I had a daughter, to be close to her, to be her friend. And I thought if we could just try this . . ." She stops crying suddenly. "Oh, my. Look at me."

She gets up and goes to the sink, like there is some sudden emergency over there. But she just wants a way to have her back to me. There she is, all dressed up like she is every day, standing around in her kitchen with no place to go. I feel sorry for her. She is just a bad mother who doesn't mean to be.

"Mrs. O'Connell?"

When she turns around, I hear myself say, "I'll tell you what. I'll come to the camp-out, too. Cynthia and I can give it a try together."

"Oh, Katie, really? That would be wonderful."

My brain is reeling. But I have a plan. A compromise. Cynthia and I go to the camp-out. Afterward, we say, that was very nice, but Scouts are not for us, okay? Then at least Mrs. O'Connell will get something and we don't lose too much.

Mrs. O'Connell may feel all cheered up, but I am full of dread. I go down the hall toward Cynthia's room on feet that would like so much to go in the opposite direction. I open the bedroom door. There is her upturned face, already full of relief. "Did you get me out?" she asks, and I say, "Not exactly."

I tell her what happened. If she were to say, "With friends like you, who needs enemies?" I would understand. But she doesn't.

Instead, she hangs her head down and says softly, "I knew it." Which is worse. I feel huge, like a hairy giant. I have no idea where to put myself.

Cynthia looks up at me and smiles. Shrugs. "Oh, well."

Bingo, forgiven. I sit down on the floor beside her and we start looking at magazines and not saying one word, only just occasionally pointing at something we know the other will understand.

I CAN'T BELIEVE IT. There it is. The place where I used to live. After Belle and Cherylanne picked me up at the airport and we came back to their house, I put my bag in Cherylanne's room and didn't even unpack—Cherylanne and I were eager to go out and take a walk so we could talk in private. But first we are just standing in front of my old house.

"I never did this before," I say.

"Did what? Spied?"

"I'm not spying!" I laugh, and Cherylanne looks a little hurt.

"I don't know what else you'd call it," she says, sniffing, and I start to answer back and then think, oh, let her have it.

"When you stand outside a house that is not yours looking in, that's calling spying," Cherylanne says.

"What I meant," I say, "is that I never got to see a place again after I left it." It seems so funny to me that my house is still there, looking just like it did when I lived there, only I don't live there anymore.

"Do you want to ask if you can look inside?" Cherylanne says. "They're real nice. They're *messy*, but they're real nice."

I think about this, then shake my head no. I would like to see the rooms again, but they would be all different now, and I think that would bother me. This is the last place my mother lived, and I don't want to see it changed. But I do appreciate seeing the outside again, the porch steps where I sat so many summer afternoons, the little strip of garden that runs along the front, the mailbox with its spot of rust that looks like a big comma.

Then, as I stare at the outside, the inside rooms start coming into my mind like waves that just cannot be stopped. I see my bedroom, the wall next to my bed where I used to make shadow puppets, the floor underneath the bed where I kept my Halloween candy and where I used to go to think things over, or to hide. Diane's room was always so neat and full of interesting things—tubes of red lipstick, pictures of Elvis, letters locked up in her jewelry box. We all lived there, our whole family, with my mother alive and all of our things in the same place. It feels so sad and marvelous to me.

I think of the bathroom where I shaved my legs for the first time, and the mirror I used to stare into, wishing for so many things. I think of the living room, the green chair in the corner where my mother sat at night to do her sewing. I see her biting off the end of the thread, the television screen reflected in her glasses. I see her bedroom, her lying under the covers with a library book propped up on her stomach, her brow furrowed with how much she was believing every word she read. She used to love reading. I see the kitchen, the way she folded towels at the table, and I see us all gathered there again for just a normal dinner, the flowered tablecloth, the round, cut-glass salt and pepper shakers, a stick of yellow butter on a saucer.

I remember the time I fell off a clothesline pole I was hanging from and knocked the breath out of myself, and I came running into the kitchen to find her, I was so scared. She pulled me onto her lap and put her hand on top of my head, and my breathing came back like a miracle. She was wearing the apron with ruffles around the edges and the heart-shaped pocket on it; I remember this now as though it just happened. Her hands smelled like lemons. I think, Every room in this house has a memory of my mother, she was everywhere in it. Then I think of the living room sofa, where she lay dying those last couple of weeks, and the day she called me to her and took my hands in hers and started to say something, but then didn't; just pushed my hair back behind my ears and smiled this so beautiful smile, *I'm all right, I'm all right.* The sun against the side of her face. Her paleness.

I swallow hard, take in a deep breath. No, I don't want to see someone else's things where she used to be. If I were a priest, I would bless this house from outside, say those beautiful Latin words that seem so red and gold, and make the sign of the cross big in the air. Instead, I just tell Cherylanne, "Let's go."

We start out down the street, and everything I see seems to talk to me, and every sentence starts with the same word: "Remember . . . ?" And inside I am answering with the most tender, *Yes, yes, yes.*

One thing I know: Anything we have, we are only borrowing. Anything. Any time.

D O YOU LIKE TEXAS OR MISSOURI BETTER?" Bubba asks. We are having dinner, and Belle has made her famous buttermilk fried chicken. Bubba has about nine hundred pieces on his plate.

"I don't know," I say. "I've kind of gotten used to Missouri, finally."

"Texas can kick Missouri's ass," Bubba says, and Belle says, "Bubba!"

Cherylanne's father is out of town and Bubba is sitting in his chair. I guess this makes him think he's the man of the house and can do whatever he wants. But he still listens to Belle; one word from her and he is suddenly very interested in his plate.

"I thought Darren was coming to dinner," Belle says, and Cherylanne's mouth turns into a tight, straight line. "He couldn't," she says.

Belle looks at her, but Cherylanne won't look back.

"Well, maybe another night," Belle says.

Cherylanne tosses her hair back. "We'll see." She is even prettier than she used to be, but I have to say I don't exactly understand what I used to find so interesting about her. All she will talk about is Darren. When I said I was thinking about college, she said the only degree a woman needed was an MRS. Then she showed me how she has started a hope chest, with some pillowcases she embroidered with hearts at the edges made out of little Xs. When I tried to tell her about the airplane trip, how it was so exciting to see the patterns in the land like giants had played in a sandbox, and how the stewardesses were so pretty and so nice, she stopped me in the middle without even knowing I was in the middle.

The phone rings, and Bubba practically knocks his chair over to run and answer it. Then, "Hey, Katie!" he yells. "It's for you!"

I feel like it's kind of rude that someone else's phone rings and it's for you, but then Belle says, "Go right ahead, honey, it's probably your dad."

"It's a girl," Bubba says, and he's kind of right; it's Ginger. "I just wanted to see how you're doing," she says.

"I'm fine," I say, and I think of how she's there and I'm here, and how different my life is from how it used to be here. I tell her a little about what we've been doing, and she tells me what she's been doing, then my father gets on and I tell him, and then there is a long silence. Finally he says, "All right, then, we'll see you at the airport the day after tomorrow. You behave," he adds.

I go back to the table and look at the familiar faces around it and I realize something: I don't live here anymore at all. Every part of me has gone from here. It's not a sad feeling, or a bad one. It's like a page turned in a notebook you will always keep, but now you are on the new page. I think something in me knew that I had to see this place again to understand that, and that is why when Fab Freddy said where, I said here.

W E ARE LYING IN CHERYLANNE'S BED just about to go to sleep, when all of a sudden I hear her burst into tears. At first I just lie still, not knowing what to do. Then I reach out my hand to turn on the bedside lamp.

"Don't!" she says, and I turn it off.

I lie back, wait for a moment, and then say softly, "What's wrong?"

"Only *everything!*"

"Darren?" I ask, and she says, "Yes."

"Well, what about him?" This afternoon when we were out walking she made him sound like the best boyfriend in the world. She said when I met him I would understand completely why she is through looking. "He is soooo cute," she said, her eyes half closed with the intensity of her emotion. "He is thoughtful and courageous and a tremendous genius. We're getting married as soon as senior year ends."

"Wow," I said, and she turned suddenly and said, "Oh Katie, if only you could meet someone like him, too."

I smiled.

"Don't worry. There's still time for you to find someone."

"I know that," I said. "There's a lot of time. For one thing, I really do want to go to college first."

She sighed. "That again. Why in the world are you so fixed on going to more school? Isn't twelve years enough?"

"I just want to go."

"But what *for?*" She pulled some leaves off a bush we walked past, then scattered them behind her as we walked. "I'm going to scatter rose petals at my wedding. Pink and ivory."

I was almost ready to tell her that I want to go to college to study poetry, but it's too important to me to risk telling anyone. So I told her I want to study anthropology.

She stopped walking. "Anthro*pology!* What's that? Just the name of it puts me in a bad mood."

"It's the study of people," I said.

"What about people?"

"Just . . . them," I said. The truth is, I don't know that much about anthropology. I just saw Margaret Mead once in a film in science class, and she seemed so wonderful. Smart and brave and so taken up with all she was doing, that distance thing in her eyes, where she was seeing something so much bigger than what was in front of her. I liked the notion of learning about how, in other parts of the world, nothing is like it is for you. Wake up in the morning, and Whoa! Different food, different shelter, different transportation, different smell to the air. Different landscape, different weather, even different light in the sky. Religions that have nothing to do with what you've been taught, jobs that are nothing you have ever seen or heard of. Women with baskets on their head, women wearing wooden shoes, women walking with goats down narrow cobblestone streets. Oxen here, penguins there. Tigers padding silently through the jungle, beneath parrots with feathers so bright and beautiful, and monkeys shrieking and hanging by one arm while they use the other one to dig in their armpit. Really, if you ever think about all that is going on in the world at any given moment, it's enough to make you stand still in wonder. And you have to think, What all happened that I am here in this place and not in another?

"Well, studying anthremology is the dumbest idea I ever heard of," Cherylanne said. "If you don't mind my saying so. I mean, going to school to learn about people, when you *are* one!"

"But there are many different types," I said. "You know, like different cultures. Have you ever heard of Margaret Mead?"

Cherylanne frowned. "What was she in?"

"In?"

"What movies?"

"She's not an actress. She's an anthropologist. Like a woman scientist."

"Well, there you go, right there is trouble," Cherylanne said. "Any woman scientist is going to be one ugly and bitter woman."

I sighed, turned my head away from her to look at the playground we were walking past. A bunch of kids laughing, having fun. I thought of the night Cynthia and I went to the school playground and rode the merry-go-round under the stars. I asked her that night to tell me honestly if she thought I could ever be famous, and she said, Yes, her face serious and true. Then she asked me if I thought she could be, and I said, Yes, too.

"If you start messing around with science, it's a cinch you're going to have a very hard time catching a husband," Cherylanne said. "One thing men do not enjoy is a woman with too many brains. Their feminine allure is sucked right out of them, and they often have bad breath. They have no idea at all how to dress, especially shoes. If you are a scientist, you will be a spinster and you will die unfulfilled, if you know what I mean. You don't want that. Believe me, it is not too soon to start living your life in such a way as to guarantee finding a good husband. Darren came to me accidentally that's true, but also, I was ready."

She kept talking, but I stopped listening. I was thinking about what my life might be like if I were a spinster. I would like to have a husband, but if I don't, maybe it wouldn't be so bad. You could live in your own house with whatever furniture and dishes and things that you picked out. You could do whatever you wanted,

with no one saying, Now *what* time are you coming home? I imagined myself living somewhere alone. There I was, in a room with
cheerful yellow walls, sunshine streaming in through the windows.
There was my cat, a handsome gray tabby, curled up on my lap as I
worked at my rolltop desk. I used thick, cream-colored paper and a
black fountain pen with a gold tip. An idea for a poem appeared
like an exotic creature peeking out from behind the bushes, and I
wrote it down, then sat quietly before it, sipping tea and smiling.

I needed to nearly cover my mouth from the excitement of the
thought. It seems like sometimes you know some things about your
life in the future even though you're only a kid, and this is one
thing I know: If I could be a poet, I would not mind living alone. I
just don't think so.

But now here is Cherylanne lying in the bed sobbing away,
saying she doesn't know what to do, she can all of a sudden feel
Darren getting cool toward her, he is just not as interested as he
used to be, and this after she has gone ahead and done it, but don't
tell anyone.

"Done what?" I ask.

"*It!*" She raises her head to look at me. Her lashes are all wet
and spiky with tears.

I gasp. "You did *that?*"

She nods.

"Did it hurt?"

"A little."

"But did you like it anyway?"

She nods again, half smiles, then lies back and starts crying
again.

I start to say something, but can't. I think of preachers I've seen
standing up high behind their pulpits, waving around their Bibles
and yelling, "*Fornication,*" the flesh of their fat chins shaking.
That's now how I feel about what Cherylanne has done. I don't
think she's committed a big sin and hurt God. I just feel sorry for

her that she doesn't have any better ideas. She reminds me of those horses tied up to a metal spoke, their heads down as they go around and around and around.

Cherylanne sits up and rubs angrily at her eyes, wiping away the tears. "I don't care what anybody says about what we did, we're practically officially engaged!" I try to think of Cherylanne and Darren going all the way, but all that comes into my head is a picture of Belle standing in the kitchen, holding a dishtowel down at her side and saying, Oh, Cherylanne.

SEATED NEXT TO ME ON THE AIRPLANE going home is a businessman, his head thrown back and snoring so loud I'm surprised the window isn't rattling. He got the window seat and he isn't even looking outside. But when I lean forward, I can see around him. There's nothing but clouds, but they are so grand, huge and puffed out and right *there*.

I never did get to meet Darren. Cherylanne felt so bad, and I didn't want to tell her that meeting Darren was not my main goal in coming, because I thought it would make her feel worse than she already does. So I said I'd meet him next time, although probably there will not be a next time. It seems so amazing to me that I used to want to be just like her, and now I don't want to be like her at all.

I remember once when we were moving, driving across country, and it was raining so hard, the windshield wipers going fast and squeaking, and then: nothing. It stopped. I looked out the window ahead of me and it was clear. I looked out the back and there was the rain, still going. Nobody said anything, but there it was, a near miracle, a rain line, a way of seeing just where something starts, when usually you are just in the middle of it before you notice it. That's how it feels to me now, to not want to be like Cherylanne anymore. I see the line.

The businessman snorts so loud, he wakes himself up. He

moves his mouth around to unstick everything. Then he looks over at me and says, "Was I snoring, little lady?"

I smile.

"I'm sorry," he says.

"That's all right."

"Tell you what, why don't we trade seats? I'll bet you'd like the window."

"Okay." We stand up and trade, and the part where we bump bodies is a little embarrassing. "Excuse me," we both say. But then I settle in and look down the whole way home and I feel like I'm seeing the best movie ever. The clouds break and I can see little toy cars on ribbons of highways. The shine of a long, crooked river. Big square blocks of buildings, the tops of trees, dots of turquoise where people have pools. I wish I could have told Cherylanne about flying, how much I like it. How you can look at the big wing of the plane outside your window and think, *What if I were riding out there*, and give yourself the shivers. But I feel too that you can just have your own storehouse of things. Someday when I'm in math class I'll be able to pull out the memory of looking down after we had just taken off and seeing a whole flight of birds traveling across the sky, their wings moving together like they had a conductor.

When I come off the plane, I see Ginger and my father right away. Ginger hugs me and then my father does. My father does it too. It's the first time. I walk so straight and careful out to the car. I sit on my knees in the backseat and look out the rear window, my way of getting some privacy. I feel so much happiness and so much sadness. My father asks if I'm glad I went back to Texas and I say yes. In my mind, I see once more the house where we lived, only I see it from high up like I'm back on the airplane. The image grows smaller and smaller, and then it is gone. I turn around, headed for the home I have now.

I ONCE OVERHEAD TWO WOMEN in a restaurant talking about vacation. One was saying to the other that it just wasn't worth it. "I know what you mean," the other woman said. "You come home and you have four times the amount of work to do."

Now I know what they were talking about. I am doing double duty baby-sitting today: first the Randolphs, and right after that, the Wexlers. And the Wexlers are going out somewhere fancy and they won't be home until really late. The good thing is that Mrs. Wexler said if I wanted to, I could have a friend over. So Cynthia will come, and we will have Loser Girls Who Never Date Have a Party with Popcorn.

It is such a fine day, that kind that makes people in good moods. Not hot, not cold, just that perfect temperature where you can't really feel any temperature, you have to move your arm around to know you're out in the air. I find some yellow and white wildflowers growing at the base of a telephone pole and I pick a few for Mrs. Randolph. When Mr. Randolph opens the door, he notices them right away and it makes him smile. I don't think there are many men who would pay attention to flowers, but Mr. Randolph is one who does. He takes the little bouquet from me to put into water, and I head down to the bedroom.

"There she is," Mrs. Randolph says. "How was your trip, dear?"

"It was good."

"What's that?"

"It was good!"

"Oh, I'm glad. Traveling is wonderful; it enriches the soul. We used to go to Europe every year before I got sick. I'll show you pictures, if you like."

"I would like to see them." Europe! I think, and that song comes in my head, *There's a place in France, where the women do a dance.* . . . I kind of want to ask if there really is such a place where women dance like that, but of course that would be such a dumb question. This happens to me all the time, really, that I see or hear something and there is this raring up of a desire to know all these other things about it. Like once in art class, the teacher showed a picture by the artist Gauguin, who went to Tahiti. And she talked a little about the painting, but I wanted to know other things, too. Like, where is Tahiti, really? I can find it on the globe, but where is it *really*? Like, how does it feel to be there? And why did Gauguin go there? How did he get there? How long did it take and what did he think when he took his first step onto that land? What kind of clothes did he wear when it was just a regular day? What did he eat for breakfast, and did he have a wife and children? Where did he get his paints in Tahiti, and what did he talk about with the person he got them from? What was his favorite color? How long did he paint at a time, and what was the first thing he did with the painting when he was done? Was he short or tall? I looked him up in the encyclopedia, but of course it did not exactly answer all these things. It happens all the time that I want to ask questions like a machine gun, but I am too shy. Plus, it can be dangerous: Ask too many questions in school and you can get a reputation for being a weirdo.

I have just gotten out the supplies for Mrs. Randolph's bath when Mr. Randolph comes in with the flowers I picked, arranged in a jelly jar. He shows his wife and she acts like it's the huge bouquet of roses Miss America carries down the runway after she wins, crying to beat the band, with her crown usually crooked. "Where are these from?" she asks, and I tell her I found them at the side of the street.

"Ah," she says, and gets that glassed over, kind of longing look.

"It's really nice today," I tell her. "Not hot at all. Maybe you'd like to go out."

"Oh, I don't know. I don't know." She looks sadly up at me.

Mr. Randolph goes out to the kitchen and I start Mrs. Randolph's bath. This is how we do it now. I do everything but the back part; then he comes and I hold her over while he does her back. He puts lotion on her at the end and she always says, "Oh, that's nice, thank you, sweetheart." Every day.

I take off her glasses and hand her the washcloth. This part she can do—she washes her face and I wash her glasses. It makes you feel so tender to see someone wash their face with such trembling hands and then hand you back the washrag, looking up at you like they're waiting for you to grade them. You want to say, "Great! You did a good job!" but that might make them feel bad that they only get complimented now on how they wash their face. So you just smile. Sometimes Mrs. Randolph has messed up her eyebrows when she washes, and now I am comfortable enough that I can make them lie back down again.

Today, after she hands me back the washcloth, she puts her hand on my arm and says, "Tell me, Katie, do you think you could do my hair for me?"

This would be a true challenge. But I could try pin curls. I tell her yes, and she gets so happy. I guess when you are in bed all day, little things become big. "But I think we have to get you in the wheelchair for that," I say. "We can bring you out to the kitchen and use the sprayer to wash your hair."

"Yes, all right," she says. "Today is good day; I think I can be up for a while."

I am actually a little excited; I have always wanted to be a beautician for a day. Whenever I see them in the shops, it looks so fun: ratting people's hair up, spraying when you're all done so it will stay, taking off their capes with a flourish. I will make a cape out of a sheet for Mrs. Randolph. I will make little curls all around her face. Maybe she has some makeup. We won't let Mr. Randolph see. *"Before,"* I will say, and send him to the store. And then when he comes back, I will show him Mrs. Randolph and say, *"After."* Maybe we will say it together.

"We'll get you all fixed up," I say, and I think she can read my mind because she says, "My niece sent me a new navy blue bed jacket—I think I'd like to wear it today."

When Mr. Randolph comes to do Mrs. Randolph's back, I tell him about the plan to get her up in the wheelchair. "I don't know," he says, quietly. "Last time didn't go so well."

One thing about people who don't hear well is sometimes they all of a sudden do. "Now, Henry," she says. "We mustn't let one bad day ruin all the rest. I want to get up so Katie can wash my hair. In fact, if it's not hot out, I might just go outside."

"Well!" Mr. Randolph raises his eyebrows and winks at me. Sometimes I feel like we are the parents and she is our child, and it is so cute. Probably sometimes she feels like that too. And then it's not so cute. She was a librarian, she told me last time. And he was a teacher. Imagine if she were twenty-one and standing in the stacks in that beautiful churchy light of libraries, and someone came up and said, "You'll end up bedridden. Your husband and a teenager will help you get washed every day." I guess it's good we don't know our own futures.

"We still read together," Mrs. Randolph told me that day. "I do one page, Henry does the next."

"Do you ever read poetry?" I asked, and she said, "Oh, my, *yes.*" My brain jerked its head up and tried to say, Hey, why don't you bring her some of your poems? but I wouldn't let it.

MRS. RANDOLPH LOOKS BEAUTIFUL, if I do say so myself. After we got her hair washed, Mr. Randolph went out for groceries. He'll be so surprised when he gets back. I put up Mrs. Randolph's hair with bobby pins, and since it's so thin, it dried right away. I made little curls all around the side of her face just like I dreamed of and ratted up the back just a little for height. We found some rouge and lipstick in her dresser drawer, and an old cake type of mascara with the little brush. It is one thing to put makeup on yourself, and another thing altogether to put it on someone else. It took me a few times, and thank goodness she had cleansing cream to wipe off my mistakes. One thing Mrs. Randolph still has are the most beautiful blue eyes, a dark blue that I have never seen before. And with the new bed jacket, they were even better. When I was all done and showed her in the mirror, she said, *Oh my!* and laughed, so I think she likes how she looks.

"How about we wait for your husband outside on the porch?" I say.

Mrs. Randolph puts her hand up to her throat, thinks for a minute. Then she nods and says, "Yes. I would like that."

As soon as we get outside, Mrs. Randolph gets very quiet. I think she is just taking in the wide world that she hasn't seen for a long time. "Well, you're right, it is a very nice day," she says. "My goodness. Birds."

And now here comes Mr. Randolph pulling up to the curb and getting out of the car with his bag of groceries. He stops about halfway up the sidewalk and just stares at his wife.

"Hello, Henry," Mrs. Randolph says. She may be in her eighties, and he may have been her husband for a long, long time, but she is flirting. And her husband is a dead duck. He just keeps looking, and then he comes up slow and kisses his wife on the forehead. "Let me just get the groceries in and I'll come out here and sit with you," he says. "I'll be right back."

As soon as he goes in, Mrs. Randolph turns to me and smiles. "He likes how I look," she says, and I say, Yes. She raises one of her trembly hands to feel the curls at the side of her face. And then, "You know, I might not mind a little ride around the block."

"Okay," I say. "I'll go tell your husband. Are you all right out here alone for a minute?"

"I'm just fine."

I go inside to ask Mr. Randolph if he would like to come and I am so surprised to find him sitting at the kitchen table, his hands over his face, his shoulders shaking.

I walk slowly up to him. "Mr. Randolph?"

He stops right away and looks up, embarrassed.

"Are you okay?"

"It's nothing," he says, and then, "She's such a beautiful woman, Katie, isn't she?"

"Yes, sir."

"Inside and out, all her life."

"Yes, sir."

He looks at me for a long moment. Then he says, "People will tell you not to get old. Has anyone ever told you that?"

"No, sir. Not yet."

"Well, they will, believe me. Someone will one day say that very thing to you. But don't you believe them. Because every day, no matter what, there's something that . . . especially if . . ." He stops, smiles. "Well, I guess I just can't say it."

"I know what you mean, though," I say.

"Do you?"

"Yes, sir."

For a moment, I get nervous that he'll want me to explain. But he doesn't. He understands that the truest things are spoken in silence.

MRS. WEXLER IS DRESSED TO THE NINES, which is what they say, although I don't get it. She's in a floor-length turquoise formal, little circles of rhinestones at each shoulder. Her hair is up high on her head, and she wears blue eye shadow to match the dress. Her purse is turquoise too, shaped like a long envelope, and it has a rhinestone clasp. But her face is tight and unhappy. "Come with me, Katie," she says, and I follow her on her blue high heels into the kitchen.

"I bought a few things for you and your friend," she says. No kidding. On the table are a whole pack of Snickers bars, Jiffy Pop, licorice, two bags of potato chips, a large bag of peanut M&Ms, and two six-packs of Coke.

"Wow," I say. "Thanks!"

"You're welcome. The boys are upstairs getting changed. I want them in bed by nine-thirty at the latest."

"Okay."

She sighs and sits down at the kitchen table, which looks so odd, you don't often see someone dressed like that sitting at a kitchen table. "So what do you think you'll do?" she asks.

"You mean . . . ?"

"You and your friend."

"Oh! I don't know, just talk, and watch TV, probably."

I am a little nervous, because when I told Cynthia to come

over, she said, "Oh boy, we can snoop," and I'm wondering if somehow Mrs. Wexler found out. But it's not that, because she says, "Well, I'll tell you, I wish I could stay here with you."

I laugh.

"I mean it," she says. And then she looks up at me like she's wondering whether she should say this or not. And she decides yes, because she says, "I hate these events. Twice a year, we have to do this with my husband's company, and I just *hate* it."

"Oh," I say. I don't know what to do. I look at the spread of treats on the table and wish it were hours later and Cynthia and I were diving into them and I was telling Cynthia how strange Mrs. Wexler is.

And then Mr. Wexler comes into the room, all clean-faced and excited, smelling of a lime-scented men's cologne, and Mrs. Wexler drags herself out of the chair. "Have a nice time," I say, and Mr. Wexler says, *"Thank you!"* but Mrs. Wexler says nothing. Because she's already said it.

THE WEXLER BOYS AND I ARE PLAYING Who Can Cheat the Most at Monopoly, a game we just made up. It started when I saw David not give enough rent money to Henry. So when it was time for me to pay David, I gypped him. He didn't get mad, he just laughed. Now things have gotten so bad we are just stealing handfuls of money from the bank, taking hotels off peoples' property and putting them on our own, skipping jail even when we get the card that says we have to go, yelling, "Twelve!" when we roll three. I have to admit we are having a good time. Really, Monopoly is not such a good game for these boys, but I prefer it to their usual, Let's See If Someone Can Get Killed. And luckily, it takes a long time, because now it is almost their bedtime. They each had a Snickers bar and a Coke, and it has made them such live wires I can't believe they'll really go to sleep, but at least they'll be out of the way.

Just as I was saying, "Okay now, this will be your last turn," the doorbell rings. "I'll get it, I'll get it," the boys all yell, and run to the door. David yanks it open so hard he knocks Mark down, and instead of saying, "Oh, sorry, are you okay?" he says, "Stupid idiot! Get *up!*" And Mark does, rubbing his elbow, but not really complaining. This is the way of boys.

It is Cynthia standing there, and I see she has a copy of *Photoplay*. We will have a good time looking at that—we have a routine where we pick a star to be and then see in the magazine if there's anything about us. No fair being anyone on the cover, of course. Or Elizabeth Taylor. Mostly we say things like, "You be Connie Francis; I'll be Sandra Dee." But for now the boys are staring at Cynthia like she is the most interesting thing they ever saw. This always happens at bedtime with kids—everything becomes something they just can't tear themselves away from.

I invite Cynthia in and say, "Okay, kids, you need to brush your teeth again and go to bed," but they just stand there in a knot of boys, not moving.

"We're playing Monopoly," Henry says. "Want to play?"

"*She* can't play now, we're in the *middle,*" Mark says, and looks at David to see if he's right.

"That's okay, we can start over," David says, and I say, "No, we can't. You guys have to go to bed."

"What's that magazine?" David asks Cynthia.

"This?" she says, holding it close to her chest. "Nothing."

"It's *Playboy!*" Mark says.

Well, I wonder how he knows what that is and what he thinks a couple of girls might be doing with it. Him saying *Playboy* feels almost like he's saying a swear.

"Okay. Time for bed." I start for the stairs, say, "Let's go," but no one comes. "Boys?" I say, and Cynthia says, "You have to go to bed, now."

"What are you guys going to do?" David asks.

"Nothing," Cynthia says. "Just keep each other company."

"Ho, you're going to look at naked *women.*" David says, and I say loudly, "Okay, that's it. Upstairs." Henry comes, and I'm so grateful for this. David and Mark are still glued to the spot, staring at Cynthia.

"How old are you?" David asks, and Cynthia says, "I'm thirty."

This is a good one, but they don't laugh; they actually believe her. "You are?" Mark says, and Cynthia says yes.

92

And then it's like they feel if she's that old, they'd better behave, and they start upstairs. I give Cynthia a look of pure gratefulness and go upstairs to supervise teeth-brushing, which consists of each of them trying to spit on each other's heads. And then they are in their bedrooms and I am free.

In the living room, Cynthia is cleaning up the Monopoly game, which is the kind of friend she is.

"Thirty years old!" I say, and Cynthia smiles. "I wonder what it's like to really be thirty," she says. "I'm so sick of being fifteen. Aren't you?"

"I'm not fifteen," I say, and Cynthia looks up at me quickly. "You're not?"

"No."

"Fourteen?" she says.

Well, I guess we have never discussed this. "I'm thirteen and a half," I say.

She sits back on her heels. "I thought you were the same age as I am. How can you be thirteen and in tenth grade?"

"I skipped a grade," I tell her, "and I also started first grade when I was five. My mother thought I was ready. Since I was going to be six in December, they let me." I feel like I'm in trouble. I feel like suddenly I'm even younger than I am.

"Huh!" Cynthia says, and I think, Here it comes, she won't want to be my friend anymore. Cherylanne was almost three years older. We really only became friends because we lived next door to each other and it was convenient. Plus I was mostly Cherylanne's slave and fan club. But then Cynthia says, "Well, you seem like you're fifteen."

I have to hold back a smile of relief. "You want to see what Mrs. Wexler left us?" I'll let her pick what to eat first, to reward her.

THE PHOTOPLAY WAS NOT A GOOD ONE. I was Debbie
Reynolds and I was nowhere; Cynthia was Doris Day and all
there was for her was just an ad for one of her movies. The
most interesting thing was the Modess ad because Cynthia and I
tried to think what came after the *because* . . . which is always
written in such feminine script. "Because . . . you can never tell I
have it on," is what they meant, we decided. You would die if
anyone ever knew you had one on. Even though all women *have*
one on several days a month. You just don't want to think about it.
Like everybody goes to the bathroom, but you do *not* want to think
about Marilyn Monroe on the toilet reading a magazine. You only
want to think about her in her sparkly clothes with her blond hair
a little over one eye. Blue eye shadow.

There is nothing good on TV. We ate popcorn and candy until
we were stuffed. Now we are sprawled out on the sofa, just staring
straight ahead. "Want to snoop now?" Cynthia asks, yawning.

"I don't know." I don't really think it's such a good idea.

"Are the boys asleep?"

"Probably."

"Well, go see," she says.

I go upstairs and peer into both bedrooms and, miraculously,
they are all asleep. There is the sound of some really deep
breathing coming from Mark and David's room; I think they are

both junior snorers. Henry is lying with his bear in his arms, his covers all tangled around his legs. I want to cover him properly, but I don't want to wake him up. I wonder if real mothers ever have this dilemma.

I come back downstairs and Cynthia says, "Well?"

I nod.

"Okay! So . . . where should we look?"

I shrug.

She looks at me. "What's the matter? Don't you want to?"

I don't say anything.

She sighs. *Thirteen*, I hear her thinking. "What time are they coming home?"

"Around midnight."

"Well, it's only ten-thirty! I always snoop when I baby-sit; it's the only thing that makes it worthwhile. Nothing *so* private. Just a little."

"Okay," I say. "But you lead."

Cynthia looks around the living room. "I don't think there's anything here," she says. "The good stuff is usually in the bedroom."

"I'm not going in there."

"Why not?"

"What if they come home, or the kids hear us?"

"It's way too early for them to come home. And if the kids hear us, we just run out in the hall and say we were checking on them."

"All right," I say. I have a nervous feeling in my stomach, but I guess that's part of the fun.

We tiptoe upstairs and go into the Wexler bedroom. Mrs. Wexler's closet is still open, and things are hung all messy in there. The bed is made crooked. Ginger would frown at this. There is a long dresser with a doily on it and some dusty pictures in frames. On a lacy metal tray, there are many bottles of perfume.

Cynthia slides open a drawer and says, "Here's her underwear."

She pulls out a pair of lacy blue underpants and waves it around. I start laughing and she says, "Shhhh!"

She opens the drawer below, pulls out a nylon stocking, and waves that around, although really it is not worth waving, it is only boring brown. I go to the other side of the dresser and open the top drawer. His socks, that's all. But there is an envelope pushed way to the back, and I pull it out. It's a little tan-colored one. There is nothing written on it. I start to put it away, and Cynthia whispers, "What's that?"

"I don't know."

"Open it!" she says, and then when I just stand there, she takes the envelope from me. Inside is a photograph. She pulls it out, and her eyes widen and she covers her mouth. "Oh, my God," she says, all muffled.

"What? What is it?"

She holds it up. It is Mrs. Wexler with no clothes on, lying on top of this very bed. You can see everything. She has a smile on her face like she feels a little sick, her eyes are almost closed. You can see *everything*.

"Maybe *this* is why her kid was talking about naked ladies!" Cynthia says. "Maybe they've found *this!*"

"I hope not. That's their mom."

Cynthia's eyes widen. "Are you kidding?" She looks at the photo again. And then we hear the door open. There is a pause, and then I hear, "Hello? Katie?" Mrs. Wexler. The naked one.

We put the photo back fast, close the door, and come out into the hall. My heart is beating so fast, I can feel it in my throat. "Just go down like normal," Cynthia whispers. "Let me go first. I'll talk."

We come downstairs and Mrs. Wexler is standing there looking at us with a question in her eyes.

"Hi, I'm Cynthia. We were in the bathroom."

Well, why did I let her talk. In the bathroom! Together!!

But, "Oh," Mrs. Wexler says, mildly. And then she turns to her husband. "I'm going to bed." It is so cold and mean, and it makes everything so uncomfortable.

"Fine," Mr. Wexler says.

I get it, I think. They had a fight. That's why they're home early. And that's why they aren't paying attention to anything else. Sometimes someone else's misfortune is your good luck.

Mr. Wexler pays me what I would have made if they'd stayed out later. "This is too much," I say, but he says, "No, you go ahead and take it. Thank you."

"Thank *you*." I feel so bad for him, his tie all loosened, his party wrecked. He goes to a high cupboard in the kitchen and takes down a bottle, then calls, "We'll see you next time."

"The boys were fine," I say, and he says good, that's good. I have a sudden thought to tell him that there is a nice men's cologne called Brut, which Bubba practically bathes in, but I don't say anything. I just close the door behind Cynthia and me as softly as I can.

IT IS ODD BUT TRUE that one of my best friends is an old priest. I met him soon after I moved here, and even though my family doesn't go to church, I go to see Father Compton every now and then. He's a white-haired guy bent over like the letter C, his eyebrows all tangled up. There is something about him that makes you feel it's all right to bring out your feelings, no matter what they are. We talk in his office, which has red carpet and dark bookcases spilling over with books, books, books. He has a little teapot and a china cup the light comes through, and he always has treats, which are supposed to be for him but he shares them with everybody.

Today he is offering me gingersnaps, which are among my favorite, so I take a couple while I tell him about what happened at the Wexlers. It is not something I could tell any other adult, but when you tell Father Compton, it is almost like talking to a stuffed animal who had lived on your bed forever. I feel so strange about what I saw, and to tell the truth I'm not sure I can baby-sit there anymore. But how to tell my dad the reason I want to quit? This is what I need help with.

Father Compton listens to the story while he eats his cookie. Little crumbs fall all over the front of him, but he pays no attention, because that is the kind of listener he is. When I'm through talking, he says, "Well, Katie, this is what I think. I think you have seen some evidence of a man who finds his wife beautiful. I don't find that so much of a problem. What concerns me is the way that you found that photograph."

I have to say that I had hoped that we could gloss over the sin of me snooping and move right into the sin of the photograph. If the photograph is not a sin, I am not so comfortable being here anymore. "Uh huh," I say, and look out the window behind Father Compton's head. Some people can tell time by where the sun is in the sky.

"We all have things we need to keep to ourselves," Father Compton begins, and I give up on looking out the window and lean back to listen to him because, as usual, he is right. Sometimes I think that when I come here to talk, my one self is saying it's for a certain reason, but my other self knows better. It waits until we get here and then it jumps out and says, *Now.*

I GUESS I HAVE STARTED A FAD, because now Ginger is entering a contest. It is something she found in a magazine, the Instant Tender Tea Contest. If she wins, she'll get Mrs. Webley for a year. Mrs. Webley is a maid who will do everything for you, so you can live the life of Riley. "Can you imagine?" Ginger says. "A maid, for a *year!* She'll cook, she'll clean, she'll baby-sit. . . ." We are lingering over breakfast. My dad has gone to work, and I don't have to work at all. What I'm going to do is go for a long walk by myself, and I'm bringing my notebook. This is something I love to do. There is a peace that comes.

"I don't need a baby-sitter," I say quickly.

"Oh, I know that," Ginger says. "But suppose your father and I wanted to take a little weekend trip. She could stay with you."

"I can stay alone!"

"I know you can," Ginger says, but she doesn't exactly sound convinced.

"I can!"

She looks up and smiles, *Okay.*

To win the contest, all you have to do is complete the last line of their jingle:

Just the top tender leaves from the top of the tree
Go into new Instant Tender Leaf Tea
The tea in this jar
Tastes better by far

_____.

That's it. You finish the jingle and send it with the inner seal from the jar. I have never told Ginger I like to write poetry, but now might be the time. "I can probably help you," I say. But then, rather than say, "I write poetry," I say, "I like poetry." It just changes like that, on the way from my brain out of my mouth.

"Do you? Oh, that's wonderful, let's do it right now. I have to go and get groceries later; I'll buy some tea and then I'll mail the entry right in—the deadline is in a week." She goes to the kitchen drawer for paper and pencils, then sits at the table with me and stares into space, thinking.

I read the ad again, study the jingle. They give a suggestion for a last line: *That's why New Instant Tender Leaf Tea is for Me!* Not to be rude, but I think Bones and Bridgett could come up with something better than that.

On my paper, I write, "Sea, glee, bee." Then, "majesty, honesty."

"What have you got so far?" Ginger asks. Her paper is blank.

"Oh, these are just words that rhyme," I say.

She comes over, looks at my list. "Hey! We could say, 'When I drink it, I feel like Her Majesty!' "

"Uh huh." I was thinking of something a little better.

"Or, 'It's the tea that just fills me with glee!' "

Uh oh, I think. But, "Maybe," I say. And then, "How about we work alone and then see what we each come up with?"

"Well, I didn't get too far before, working alone," Ginger says. "I *like* this idea of working together!"

"Or . . . ," I say, my eyebrows all wrinkled like this brilliant idea is just occurring to me now. "You could go get the tea and I could come up with some things, and then you could just pick the one you like best."

"That would be perfect!" she says, and she is as smiley as a little kid handed a yellow balloon.

I LIKE WHEN YOU WALK FAR ENOUGH that a kind of relaxation happens and you can be inside the rhythm of your feet. Your brain shifts like a car; you settle down, look around, and feel *ah*. In a more slow-motion way, you see where you are. And where I am is outside and free, on a summer day. There are times you know your own luck.

The thing about seasons is that when you're in one, you can't believe the others will ever come back. It feels to me like summer has its feet planted far apart and its hands on its hips: *I am here*. Gardens are full of primary colors, grass sprouts from cracks in the sidewalk, bees fly heavy and low, like you could just reach down and grab one. You can smell the heat trapped in the concrete, that ironed pillowcase smell. Windows are open, and people seem open too—there is no hunching over from the cold, keeping your eyes on the sidewalk, concentrating on getting to where you're going so you can be warm and not freeze to death. When you pass by someone, you take the time to nod a greeting or even stand and have a little conversation, the sun making a disc of warmth on the top of your head.

Curtains move in S-shaped dances from the breeze, or puff out dramatically, then fall straight and still, like they're denying they did anything. Kids with Kool-Aid mustaches run in and out of the house, banging the screen door and yelling to their mothers, and you can hear the faint voice of their mothers yelling back *not to bang the door*, how many times does she have to *tell* them to *not bang the door*. There is a different weight to the air. People sit on their porches after dinner, reading the paper or sitting idle, their hands behind their heads and their ankles crossed, waiting to see who passes by. There is a low happiness in them that they can't explain.

I walk far enough out of the neighborhood that the houses end and open fields begin. I don't know who these fields belong to. I don't see how they can belong to anyone, really, how any land can. I wonder sometimes how it all started, that land got owned. Somebody came someplace new and didn't see anybody else around and said, "Huh. Well, this is mine." And then they stuck a flag in. And then came war.

I wander far out into the middle of a field and lie down in knee-high grass. What a fine smell; you can understand why horses eat it. I close my eyes and listen to the drone of an airplane overhead. Now I have been on an airplane. It is in my bag of experiences, which mostly is empty. I wonder when I die what will be in my bag, and why. I think of Mrs. Wexler, and how her bag must be pitiful flat, and then I think of the Randolphs and how each of their bags would look like it was about to explode. I don't know, really, why it ends up that some people get so much and some so little. Some they can't help it, but some they can.

I sit up, take out my notebook, smooth the page with the flat of my hand. I want to try a poem about a summer day. I want yellow and green in it; I want heat and drops of water and the slow flap of a new butterfly's wings. I think I'll end with something I saw on the way over: a slide on a playground, the metal glinting so hard in the sun, a line of kids all waiting to go up the ladder. Whenever I start a poem, I feel like my heart is about to break. Because of all there is, because of how every single thing can have such a pure beauty that aches to be known. I take in a deep breath, and then all there is is the scritch scritch scritch of my pen, trying to say something so true. What if it works? Then when I read it again, the little voice inside will say, *Yes. Yes. Yes.* And there will be this rare excitement that makes me bend over myself with pleasure, then rise up smiling, my fingers pressed over my mouth as though to keep things from bursting out. I am lucky on the inside.

WHEN I COME BACK FROM MY WALK, Ginger is so excited to see me. "I got the last line of the jingle!" she says. "It just all of a sudden came to me at the grocery store!"

"Let's see," I say, and Ginger says, "Well, I'd like to read it to you. Will you let me read it to you?"

"Sure!" I sit down and turn toward her, my knees together and my hands in my lap like a real audience.

She moves to the middle of the kitchen, straightens, then holds up the page she's written her poem on. It's her good stationery; I can see the design of the flowers that go all around the edges. She starts to read, then all of a sudden stops. "Well, for heaven's sake, I can't believe it, I feel nervous!"

I understand this. You've done something so important that you are worried about showing someone else. It is too delicate and newborn, even if it's not new. Inside yourself, hands wring. "Want me to close my eyes?" I ask.

"No, that's okay. It's just that I've never written a poem before. But here, here goes."

She takes in a breath, then recites:

> *Just the top tender leaves from the top of the tree*
> *Go into new Instant Tender Leaf Tea*

The tea in this jar
Tastes better by far
Than French food in gay old Paree!

"Oh! . . . That's *good*," I say. How can I not. She's so proud, her mouth in a tight smile and her eyes so lit up.

"Thank you! Okay, so I guess I'll just mail it in. And then we just have to wait."

"Right." I imagine a table full of judges, all wearing those half glasses. I hope they'll be kind.

"How about some lunch?" Ginger asks.

I nod yes. And then I hear myself say, "Would you like to read a poem I wrote today?" It is as though my shy self has slipped past my guard self, and bingo, my secret is out.

"You did it, too?" She turns on the faucet, starts washing her hands.

"I didn't write anything for the contest," I say. "I wrote just . . . a poem. About summer."

"Well, read it to me, like I did to you."

"I think it might be better if you just read it to yourself."

She comes over, wiping her hands on the little towel built into her apron. I start to hand her my poem, then say, "Would you mind if I leave while you read it?"

Something in my face tells her something. "That's fine," she says, serious, and I go to my room. I know it will only take a minute for her to read, but I stay sitting on my bed for ten minutes. When I come out, she's making sandwiches. She puts plates for both of us on the table. BLTs. She pours milk for me, coffee for her. Then she sits down and looks at me, standing there in the middle of the kitchen. "I don't know anything about poetry, really," she says. I am all of a sudden so embarrassed that I showed her. But then she says, "But I know when someone has a gift. And I think you do, Katie. My goodness, you're a poet, and I never even knew."

I sit down at the table. One of my fists is clenched so tight. And in my head, a person who was out walking and walking in the dark comes to a little house with a light on. Waits at the door for a moment, and then goes in. Finds such a welcome that she stays.

MRS. RANDOLPH IS SICK. "Under the weather," Mr. Randolph calls it. At first I feel guilty, thinking I should never have taken her outside, but he says it's not that. "It happens every now and then," he says. "She'll rally. She's sleeping, now—we'll just let her rest." He pulls out a kitchen chair, gestures for me to sit down at the table, and he sits at the other side. "I thought I'd make a nice cold soup for dinner, a cucumber soup. Maybe you could help me."

Well, I have never heard of such a thing. Cold soup! And made out of cucumbers! But I just smile and nod like my family had it for dinner just last night.

Mr. Randolph lays some newspaper out on the table, then gets some cucumbers out of the refrigerator and hands them to me. "You peel, and I'll chop, okay?"

While I peel the cucumbers, he washes his breakfast dishes. I look at his skinny back, the slow, slow way he puts the dishes in the drying rack. When Ginger does dishes, she's so fast, it's like her hands are a blur. The way Mr. Randolph does it is so slow, it's interesting to watch, like a movie of something you've seen so many times, but never seen.

I think of how Mr. Randolph is so careful with everything, and then I think of the Wexlers. How can they be so different? Didn't they both feel so in love at first, and what happened to the Wexlers that they don't have that anymore?

"Mr. Randolph?" I say. "Do you and your wife ever fight?"

He turns around, smiles. "Oh, sure." He holds a cup under the rinse water, puts it in the rack. "Why do you ask?"

"Just curious."

"When we were young, we used to go round and round about all kinds of things, politics especially. We don't do that so much anymore. Now it's a little disagreement every now and then over whether the peas are too salty. But you can't have a marriage without a little conflict."

"You just seem so happy," I say.

"Well." He turns to smile at me. *Yes, we are*, he is saying. I imagine him trying to help Mr. Wexler, but all that comes into my head is Mr. Randolph hearing about how Mrs. Wexler treats Mr. Wexler, then shaking his head, saying, *Well, I'm sorry, young man.* A pat to the shoulder. *I truly am sorry for you, son.*

I'm done peeling the cucumbers by the time he's finished with the dishes. He puts a cutting board down on the table, takes the cucumbers from me, and starts chopping. "I can help do that, too," I say, and he says, "No, no need. I'm happy just to have your company."

"Oh, okay," I say, and then my mind goes plumb blank. I hate when this happens. I clear my throat, hoping for a jump start to start talking again, but it's no good.

"Happy to just have you sitting there," Mr. Randolph says, again. He hasn't even looked up, but somehow he knows what I'm thinking.

I hear the wood and knife language of his chop-chop-chopping, and the rhythm brings a kind of comfort. I lean back and let the sound fill the space. I look around the kitchen, the yellow ruffled curtains at the window, the cheerful wallpaper, the long Formica counters. This kitchen is bigger than ours, even though there's just the two of them; the Randolphs never did have children.

"Are you looking forward to classes starting?" Mr. Randolph asks.

"Some."

"Ah. So you'll be 'creeping like the snail, unwillingly to school.'"

"Who said that?"

"The bard."

"Pardon?"

"William Shakespeare."

"Oh! I've read him, a little."

"And?"

"Well, it's beautiful, his language. When I read it, I feel . . . high up. But sometimes it's hard to understand."

"You need a good teacher to really appreciate Shakespeare."

"They're hard to find," I say. "I've only had a couple good ones. But they were so—"

Suddenly Mr. Randolph stops chopping and lifts his head in a particular kind of alertness.

"Want me to check on her?" I ask, but he is already up and on his way to Mrs. Randolph's bedroom.

I follow him down the hall. She's awake. Now, how did he know? There was not one sound.

He sits on the bed beside her. I'll bet he smells like cucumbers. I'll bet she can smell that plain, clean smell from his hand that he has laid at the side of her face.

"Feeling better?" he asks, and she nods yes.

In some couples, each puts the other first.

TUESDAY AFTERNOON, Cynthia and I are playing cards on her bedroom floor. Gin rummy. Mrs. O'Connell is out of the house for once, gone to the beauty parlor, so Cynthia and I are alone. Before she left, Mrs. O'Connell gave me a little gift. A Girl Scout uniform. "Oh," I said, "you shouldn't have done this." I meant it so much. "Well, you're one of us, now," she said, in a singsong, dancey voice, and I said, "Well, no, actually I am just going to come to the camp-out. I thought I'd try that first and see how it went. Remember?"

"You're going to love it," she said. "And I got you a beret and a sash, too, but they'll take a little while—they're so popular they're out of stock!"

More like they're so unpopular they gave up on making them, I thought, but I could feel Cynthia squirming next to me, and so rather than arguing, I just thanked Mrs. O'Connell. "You're more than welcome," she said, and then she looked at her bracelet watch and gasped, "Heavens! I've got to dash," which no one but her would ever say.

"She ordered socks, too, you know," Cynthia says now.

"I'm not taking them."

"Ha. Like she'll give you a choice."

"I'm *not.* I'll just leave them here with the uniform; I'm not taking that either. After the camp-out, we'll just tell her Girl Scouts aren't for us, and she can return everything."

"We have to *wear* everything that night."

I look up from adding the numbers on my cards. "What for!? You don't wear dresses at a camp-out! She said she was going to make it like the woods."

"*After*. First we have to have an official meeting, and everyone is going to wear their uniforms. Even she is; she got a leader's uniform. She's tried it on three thousand times."

"Oh, boy," I say, and I start to get in a bad mood, but then I just start laughing, and Cynthia does, too. We throw down our cards and lie on the floor, groaning as loud as we can, having such a good time with our suffering that we almost forget to watch *As the World Turns*. We eat sour pickles while we watch it. I don't know why, really. We did the first time and then we happened to the next time and now we sort of have to. Like Christmas.

TWO MIRACLES HAVE HAPPENED. One is, Ginger won a prize for her jingle! Not Mrs. Webley, but she did win a mixer. She was so proud when she told us at dinner—she took off her apron to make the announcement. My father and I clapped, and then my father whistled between his teeth, which got the dogs fired up, and they had to be told to lie back down, and then everybody started laughing. It was one of those rare moments when I thought, Why can't it always be like this? And something in me rose up and floated over the kitchen table, taking a kind of photograph to try to preserve everything: the three of us sitting there; the smell of dinner; the low slant of late afternoon sun coming through the window to make a patch of light on the floor; dust motes spinning like a million ballerinas. I want to remember that Ginger's grin was lopsided, that the sternness in my father's face fell away, that three freckles were in a line on my left hand, that the dogs lay nose to nose, like bookends—just every single thing from this one moment. And then I can put it in the inside scrapbook, to look at when things are not going so well.

The mixer hasn't arrived yet, but Ginger has already bought a cover to disguise it. The cover is made to look like a rooster. Which I don't get, because what would a rooster be doing, sitting on your kitchen counter? But anyway, the rooster cover is lying folded in the corner, where the mixer will go. It is actually true that we are all excited for it to come, like a new person is moving into the house.

The second miracle is that the place where Mr. Randolph taught is the Bartlett School for Girls, and he wants to see if he can get a scholarship for me to go there. I cannot believe that this will really happen, but he talked to my father about it and I have an interview set up for next week. You have to have an interview to go to this school, like a job. I am already plenty worried about what to wear, how to sit, what to say. I will write to Cherylanne, because even though she's lost her mind a little, she can still help with these things. She always knows what to wear.

After dinner I go into my room to listen to Fab Freddy and to think about all that has happened in a day. It's so funny now, how when I listen to him, I feel I kind of know him. Like I could call and say, This is Katie Nash, and he might say, "Oh, yeah. How was Texas?"

During a commercial, I come out to the kitchen to get a drink of water. Out in the backyard, I see Ginger sitting on the porch steps, a cup of coffee beside her. I wonder if she's feeling bad about not being the grand-prize winner. In the living room, my dad is watching television. He would not be the best consolation if she is feeling bad. He would stand beside her, stirring up the change in his pocket.

I come out and sit beside her and she doesn't say anything, just pats my knee.

"It's nice out," I say.

"I think we've lost that terrible humidity for a while."

"I guess so." One thing adults like to talk about is humidity.

She points to a corner of the yard. "You know what's coming up over there?"

I squint, trying to see something. "No."

"Snapdragons. They took their time, but they're coming."

"What color?"

"Pink and yellow."

"Oh good." Pink and yellow are my favorite colors. The colors of cheerfulness and Easter.

"You know what I was just out here thinking about, Katie?"

"What?"

"I was thinking that I'm so glad I didn't win Mrs. Webley."

Sour grapes, they call this.

"I really mean it. I was sitting here thinking about what it would really have been like. Every morning, I'd have to get ready for Mrs. Webley. Would I have time for coffee first? Would I have to get dressed right away? You know, some days I just like to stay in my robe for a while. Sometimes I make the beds and dust and vacuum before I ever get dressed."

"I know."

"And how could I do that if Mrs. Webley was coming?"

"Well, she was supposed to do the cleaning, so you could go out."

"Yes, but . . . go out where? Oh, it might be fun the first week or so, but then I'd feel like I was getting kicked out of my own house!"

"You wouldn't have to leave. It's your house."

"But with another person coming every day, it's like it isn't your house anymore. And I realized . . . Well, I just realized how much I like my life, Katie. And how I'm so glad I'm going to get that mixer instead of Mrs. Webley."

If this is sour grapes, they're pretty sweet. I pick a fat blade of grass, rub it between my fingers. This makes the best perfume. "I wonder who did win. I wonder if they're thinking, *Uh oh.*"

"Well, exactly," Ginger says, laughing.

I lean back on my elbows, look up into the night sky. Sometimes I get this feeling of a wink coming down from the heavens to me.

After a while, the screen door bangs shut, and here comes my dad. He's heard our voices. They've called him out. Seems like summer nights just do that to a person, make you kind of sociable. There you are, watching *Rawhide*, and the voice of your wife and your daughter curl around you like pie smells in the cartoons. All he does is sit down and light up a cigarette. But it is a lot.

ON SATURDAY MORNING, Cynthia and I go to the Hill of Truth. This is a place we found on our bikes, far away from either of our neighborhoods. It's a fairly high hill; you can sit up there and feel like you're away from everything. We decided that it is the place where we will never lie to each other, not even white lies, and where important decisions will be made, such as how far we will go if we ever get boyfriends. Sometimes we talk about dumb things, like who is best, Ricky Nelson, Elvis, or Pat Boone. But most times we talk about things like what scares us the most, or what we have done in our lives that we are proud of. Moments of embarrassment, like the time Cynthia was shaking the hand of her pastor and farted. We imagine what our days will be like when we are grown women, what the furniture in our houses will look like. Who our husbands might be, and what it feels like to do it the first time, and how do you know how to do it; is it true that the sex hormones just take over and lead the way? Does it hurt so much to have a baby that you faint? We talk about what is the more important thing in a person, brains or kindness. Do plants have feelings? One time we tried to have mental telepathy with each other, but it didn't work—we sat back-to-back with our eyes closed, and I was to imagine an object in a house and Cynthia was to guess what it was. *Fork*. I was thinking, *Fork. Fork. Fork.*

"Chair?" Cynthia said. "Television? . . . Curtains? . . . Oh, I know, I know! *Rug!*"

"Forget it," I said.

Once we talked about what would we tell our children if we knew we were dying. This is something I brought up because my mother never said too much to us, and it has left me in a constant state of wondering. Cynthia said she would tell her children that she was not afraid, even if she was. I said that I would admit if I were afraid, but not in a way to make *them* afraid. Cynthia said that would be hard to do, and I said I knew that, but that I would find a way.

Once Cynthia said that sometimes she wishes her mother would die, and I just nodded, because I do understand how that can happen. I had a teacher once who used to paddle kids with a smile on her face, and she would never let you go to the bathroom, unless you had to throw up. "Did you ever wish your mother would die?" Cynthia asked. "I mean, before she got sick?"

I shook my head no.

There was a long pause, and then Cynthia said, "Katie? Did I hurt your feelings about your mother by telling you that about my mother?" I started to say no, but we were on the hill, so I said, "In a way. But only because it reminds me that it was a luxury to have her, and I didn't know it. And now it's too late." I looked over at Cynthia, shrugged.

"Do you think it's bad that sometimes I wish my mother would die?" Cynthia asked, and I said, "Not unless you kill her." Then we both started laughing and got on our bikes and went to eat butterscotch-dipped cones at Dairy Queen, which is what we always do after being on the hill. It makes you feel good to be so honest and to feel so safe about telling whatever you want, and also it makes you hungry, I don't know why.

We sat at one of the wooden tables, our bikes resting against a nearby tree, and I was watching Cynthia eat her cone and I was thinking, *This is the first time I have had a friend I was equal with*. I wanted to reach across the table to touch her hand, but the time of serious talking had passed, we were only eating ice cream, so I kept the thought to myself. Also, I kept to myself the sigh feeling that I wish we weren't such duds, that we would be going home and getting ready to go somewhere really good.

WHEN I GET HOME, I find a letter for me on the kitchen table from Cherylanne. It's the fastest response I've ever gotten from her.

Dear Katie,

Okay, first, about your interview. Wear solids. Simple earrings or no earrings at all, and I hope I do not have to tell you that things like bangle bracelets are a no-no as they are vulgar. Do not wear those white socks, your father is going to have to let you wear nylons, and be sure there are no runs. Comb your hair really well and tie it back loosely at the nape of your neck. Not a ponytail, I cannot emphasize this enough, ponytails scream NOT SERIOUS. Flats with no scuff marks. And posture, remember to keep that back straight and head held high but not conceited as I have shown you about one billion times.

Just answer the questions in the best way you can but do not go on too long because the Be Mysterious thing holds no matter what. And smile, smile, smile. But not like an idiot, just at the right places. All the time be thinking, I will succeed! because your insides must match with your outside. Keep eye contact with the interviewer but not too bold. You can best achieve this by occasionally looking away in the modest fashion, which is you look down a little.

Oh Katie, I just have to tell you something. I can't give my full attention to your question because something bad has happened which is that I am in trouble. You know. In Trouble. I have told my mother and the thing we are going to do is I am going to get married sooner than I thought. My father is hardly speaking to me and Bubba runs around saying, "I'm an uncle, I'm an uncle," which of course he isn't even, yet, and you would think he could for once in his life think about something besides himself. Darren says he still loves me but I must say he is not exactly acting like it. Like does he call every night anymore? NO. And if he did, I could tell him things like my plan of how every Friday we will have a special dinner with candles and I know that would make him feel better.

Anyway, so much is happening as you can imagine and I can't tell you all of it now. But I do ask you to keep me in your thoughts and prayers because I realize you really were a friend to me.

Well, I started out writing this letter under a cloud of gloom but it felt good to tell you things and now I feel better. Everything will work out. I hope you will let me know if you really go to a private school, which who would have thought it. I need things now to take my mind off things so I hope you get in that school and then you can gossip to me all about what rich girls are really like. I believe for one thing they all dye their hair. Plus flying off to Europe is nothing to them, believe me.

Love,

Cherylanne

P.S. No perfume. And no garlic or onions the night before. Or cabbage, good grief. And thank them for taking the time to interview you as you are leaving. One smile over the shoulder. Demure and mature.

I hold the letter in my lap and imagine Cherylanne sitting in her room, writing it. I think of how she is not a child any longer, how inside her a baby is growing. I wish I could help her, but I can't. It is so scary how all of a sudden, there you are, smack in a life of your own making. My sister, Diane, got pregnant early too, but she lost the baby. I have a feeling Cherylanne will have a strong and healthy baby, and then there she will be in some little house with Darren going to work and her staying home and looking out the window. Patting the baby. Saying, Don't you cry.

I suppose it might be a bad thing about me that next I just move back in the tips part of the letter again and start imagining my outfit. I have a matching skirt and blouse, light blue. I think of sitting there at the end of the interview, saying, "Well, thank you, I know I will love being a student here." That's because the head guy has just said "Ordinarily, Miss Nash, we take a while to decide whether or not we will admit someone. But I'm sure I speak for all of us here [he looks around at the smiling committee] when I say I would like to extend our invitation to you immediately. Am I not right, colleagues?" They all nod, clapping.

But then I think of being dropped off for the interview and walking up to a desk in the reception room of the school and a blond secretary wearing glasses on a string says, "You're who? To see whom? . . . I'm sorry, there's nothing on the calendar. Are you certain they wanted to see you?" And to herself she is thinking, "This *has* to be a mistake. For heaven's sake. This is the *Bartlett* School."

I go over to my closet, tell myself to stop thinking such things and just find the outfit. I put my hand on a hanger and then I just stand there, thinking, *Oh, Cherylanne*, I remember how she looked one day at the swimming pool, standing perfectly still on the high board before she dove off it. How her stomach was perfectly flat, just a girl's.

WHEN I RING THE WEXLERS' doorbell at seven o'clock on Wednesday night, Mr. Wexler answers in his pajamas. I step back, embarrassed. And I think he is, too. And then we both start apologizing. "I forgot all about you," he says. "I'm so sorry. The boys aren't here. They're with my sister."

I start to say I'll just come back on Friday, but he asks me to come in, it's like he's glad to have some company. I step into the hall, and he says, "Why don't you have a seat, I'll be right back."

He goes upstairs, and I start for the kitchen, then stop dead in my tracks. The sink is piled high with dirty dishes, there are beer bottles everywhere, and the garbage is overflowing. You can smell it: coffee grounds and something like cheese. On the table are newspapers and coffee cups.

I go into the living room and quickly arrange myself on a chair, so he won't know I've seen the kitchen. Not that the living room is so perfect, with his socks lying around, an ashtray overflowing with cigarette butts, the blinds pulled to make for a dreary dimness.

When Mr. Wexler comes down, he is dressed in a plaid, short-sleeved shirt and khaki pants, no shoes. No belt. He comes into the living room and sits in the chair opposite me. "Well. You must be wondering what's going on." He laughs a little.

I don't know the polite way to answer, but finally I just say, "Yes, sir."

"Mrs. Wexler is . . . she's on a little vacation. And I sent the boys to stay with my sister for a while. Just for a while, until I . . ." He sits there, staring straight ahead. Then he looks at me and says, "Until I decide what to do. The vacation may last a while. It may last quite a while. I think the boys will be better off staying where they are maybe until school starts. So I guess we won't be needing a baby-sitter."

"Oh, okay," I say. I think of Henry, my favorite, lying in a new bed and thinking about the last number. But probably he is not thinking about that, probably he is thinking, Where is my mother? This pinches my heart so hard I have to change my position on the sofa.

"Now, I know we hired you for the summer," Mr. Wexler says, "and I'm going to pay you what you would have earned if you'd worked for us."

"Oh, no," I say. "That's okay."

He holds up his hand. "I would feel much better if you'd let me."

"Well," I say. "I don't really . . . Maybe I could help you clean up a little. That way I could earn it."

He looks around as though he is seeing the place for the first time. And then he says, with a kind of dignity, "It's all right. I'll get to it."

"I could just do the dishes for you."

"Katie," he says. "Mrs. Wexler has left me."

"Yes, sir."

"I'm afraid I'm at a bit of a loss, here."

"Well, if you . . . I'd be glad to help you. I mean, clean up. I can help you do that. And also, I . . ."

"Yes?"

"Well, I just want to say I think you're a very nice man."

"Ah." He leans his head back and I get the terrible thought that it's because he's crying. And I'm right, because here come two tears rolling down his cheeks. It makes me feel so strange, like all of a sudden I have the flu. This is my summer of seeing grown-ups cry.

"Mr. Wexler?" He clears his throat and quick wipes away the tears.

"Yes?"

"Do you want to wash or dry?"

He looks at me with such gratitude it's as if I have knocked on his door and said I am from *The Millionaire*. "Dry, I guess," he says, and I tell him that's the exact right answer that I was hoping he would say.

I'M NOT EVEN IN THE BARTLETT SCHOOL, but I already have homework. I got a letter from them saying that before I meet with the people there, I have to write something on two topics of my own choosing. Right away two things popped into my head. One was something that happened with my mother, and the other was something I saw from the airplane window. So this morning I wrote an essay about the time my mother and I planted a carrot garden, only the carrots never grew. I wrote about how she came out and knelt down and took off her glasses to have a closer look at nothing. How we tried a fertilizer made from coffee grounds and eggshells. How it changed from our expecting to our hoping, to our wondering what we did wrong, to our disappointment, to our final day in the garden, when we just sat in the dirt and laughed. And how that night when everyone was sleeping I took a few carrots from the refrigerator and put them in the ground and the next day I showed her and of course she knew but she pretended she didn't. I wrote how she smiled at me that day, and how we brought the carrots in and ate them for lunch. And how the harvesting was so bountiful, and it had nothing to do with carrots.

Now I am thinking of what to say about what I saw from the airplane window. I suppose I could try an essay about that too, but it doesn't seem right, because the sight was too delicate for all those words. It seems like a poem would be the right thing. And now that

I have broken the ice by showing something to Ginger, I think I might be ready to show something to someone else. I get out my haiku notebook and stare at the white page, whisper some possibilities out loud to myself. Then I write

> *Fog at mountain's base*
> *A shallow bowl of earth holds*
> *Sky fallen from sky*

There. Close enough. I close my book, lay it on my desk. Later, I'll copy the haiku onto a separate page and submit it with my essay. I think of how judges read Ginger's poem and how now it will be my turn. I'm glad I don't have to be in the room when they do it. Imagine how time would be stretched, one second equaling one hour. An eyebrow lifts; you die.

I lie on my bed, put a pillow over my belly and hold it tight against me. "Oh, my darling," I say, out loud. To no one.

Dear Katie,

Congratulations! I had a feeling you would get in. I hope you like it there and that the kids are nice to you. I have to say I think it would be hard to go to a school with all girls, I can't even imagine wanting to do it. But good luck!

I am sending a little gift that is from my mother and me, and I know Bubba signed the card, but believe me, he had nothing to do with it, he just can't stand not being in the middle of everything with his own finger pointing to his own self. I hope you like it and that also it brings you good luck to make all A's.

I am getting married in three weeks, just a small ceremony, which of course is not what I ever thought I'd have. But you can only do so much with so little time. I am wearing white, I don't care. Only our families will be there, and then I will be Mrs. McGovern, which I still can't believe. I had a dream about the baby last night and it was a girl and it had black hair and blue eyes like Darren. The next day it seemed like it just had to be true, and it made me wonder, do mothers and unborn babies have a psychic connection?

Friends from school are being very immature about all this, which what do you expect and who cares anyway, since I will not be returning for my senior year. I wish I hadn't gotten the class ring, because what good is it now. But anyway, I will write

after the wedding to tell you all about what it was like. I am
thinking of you right now in your bedroom, where I too have
been. If I close my eyes, it can seem like I really am there, and I
wish I were to hug you and say again Congratulations!
Love,
Cherylanne
(AND her baby GIRL, I would bet one million dollars)

The gift Cherylanne sent is a silver pen-and-pencil set. It is
beautiful, with thin lines engraved on it. When you pull apart the
pencil, there is the eraser, which I will never use except in emer-
gencies, because it looks so round and perfect. When I write with
the pen, I feel myself sit up straighter, my knees and ankles
touching. Proper. I am a girl who lives on an estate, wears jodhpurs,
sleeps in a canopied bed, and whose father calls her sweetheart,
that's what this pen does.

I write a thank-you note to Cherylanne, and when I'm done, I
lie on the bed with a full feeling in my chest, and then I just start
bawling. It's because I wasn't able to say how much I love her and
Belle both, and also because I love the memory of Cherylanne and
me hanging around the PX, talking in our bedrooms, reading magazines in front of the fan when it was too hot to be outside. It feels
like now we are so much older, and our lives are diverging like
those geometry proofs where the two lines never touch, they just
keep growing farther apart. It will never happen again that we will
walk home from a movie, holding hands with each other to be the
substitute, singing "Tammy's in love" in soft, flirty voices. I feel like
I am the mother of my own self and Cherylanne too, looking down
on us as we were then, tender in the heart with knowing all that is
to come. And all I said in the letter is, "Thank you for the pen-and-
pencil set, I will use it every single day." This is why I'm crying, the
distance from what you feel to what you say, how it will always be
like that.

IT'S POURING RAIN WHEN I GO TO THE RANDOLPHS', the slanty kind that makes an umbrella pretty useless. Flowers are beaten down in their beds, and small twisted streams run at the edges of the streets. Outside one house I pass two little boys in matching yellow raincoats trying to sail boats, but they only spin and run into the curb. It makes me wonder what the Wexler boys are doing. And Mr. Wexler. And Mrs. Wexler, too. I feel like I was watching a TV show and someone came in the room and snapped it off, right in the middle. And there is no one to say "Hey!" to.

When I arrive, Mr. Randolph chuckles at my drowned look and tells me to wait in the entryway. He brings me some towels to dry off, and then I come into the kitchen. I smell chicken soup, one of Mr. Randolph's specialties. Mrs. Randolph is up in her wheelchair, sitting at the table, an untouched cup of tea and a plate of toast before her. Next to her are photograph albums, three of them. It seems she wants to show me pictures today, but to tell the truth, it doesn't look like she should be out of bed at all. I can't believe Mr. Randolph was able to get her up alone. There is a terrible weariness in her face, a breathlessness when she talks. Mr. Randolph asks if she wants to go back to bed before he goes to the grocery store, but no, she wants to stay up.

"Sit down, Katie," she tells me, and I do.

"My goodness," she says. "Is it raining that hard?"

"Yes, ma'am."

"Are you cold? Do you need a change of clothes?"

Not to be rude, but I can just see myself in one of her house-dresses.

"No thank you, I'm fine."

"Well. First of all, I want to congratulate you," she says. "Henry told me you were accepted at the Bartlett school!"

"Yes, ma'am." I don't know why, but hearing her say this I get a twist of shame in my belly.

"It's a wonderful place."

"Yes, ma'am." Where to look. I don't know. It's wilting shyness that makes me grab my thumb with my other hand and squeeze. I wish I would stop being like this.

"Did they show you around at all?"

"Yes, there was a student there, a senior, and she showed me everything. And next week, I'm going to a party with some of the other sophomores."

"Well, that's wonderful." She smiles, closes her eyes. And doesn't open them.

"Mrs. Randolph?" I say.

She starts, blinks. "Oh. I'm so sorry. I'm taking some new medication, and I'm just not used to it yet." She pulls one of the scrapbooks closer to her. "I wanted to show you some pictures of Paris," she says. "I thought you might enjoy looking at these."

I pull a chair up next to her, and she opens the first book. "This is the tiny little apartment we rented," she begins, and she is smiling. I lean over the pictures and go with her to another time, when she and Mr. Randolph were in their twenties and used to go every day to a café near the Eiffel Tower that had lace curtains and coffee cups that looked like cereal bowls. They walked down cobblestone streets past curly iron balconies full of flowers, carrying long loaves of bread with the ends bitten off. All the pictures she shows me seem unreal, not only because she and Mr. Randolph are so different now, but because the buildings and the streets are not like anything I've ever seen. It's one thing to look at Paris, France, in a textbook. It's another to see pictures of people you know living there, with their own whole life turned French, just because they decided to do it. There they are in the sweaters they bought at Sears, standing in front of the Mona Lisa herself. It doesn't seem possible.

When Mr. Randolph comes home, he looks at the pictures with us. There is one time when he glances so tenderly over at his wife. She doesn't see it, but I do, and it makes me happy, like when you see one bird feed another. Sometimes one or the other of them tells a little story about a picture that we come across. When that happens, I see a kind of movie on the page: The background expands, and I can almost hear the sounds that were there at the time the picture was taken—motorcycles gunning, or dish towels flapping on the line, or kids wearing knapsacks and shouting French things as they chase each other down the street. Looking at one photo of an outdoor restaurant, I feel the white tablecloth beneath my elbows and hear the feathery rustle of pigeons coming to land, making their matronly cooing sounds as they gently bump into each other. Outside, the rain sometimes comes down so hard, we have to talk louder, and it feels like a miracle that the roof holds. It makes for a coziness and for a gratefulness, too, that you have the choice to not be out in it. You can sit at the table and look out the window and not have to feel what you see. It seems so pure and timeless, the need for shelter, and the connection we have to cave people looking out at the weather from the entrance to their caves. Here we are, still doing it. Wearing way different things but probably feeling just the same.

I love sitting at this table with these two old people, looking at these pictures, hearing live history, smelling the soup turn more and more chickeny as it cooks on the stove. I am enjoying waking dreams from my own wandering thoughts. Feeling the slow ticktock of the day with the lazy pleasure of a cat sleeping on a windowsill in the sun. It comes to me that there isn't any place else I'd rather be. I wonder if this makes me weird.

ICANNOT BELIEVE THE HORRIBLENESS OF MY LIFE at the moment. If I had to grade it, I would give it an F triple minus, which is a grade I actually got once on a science test given by an evil teacher, Mr. Wybold. For him, a simple F wasn't bad enough. He had his own grading system, which he told us about with a big grin on his face, tossing the chalk up and down in his hand. Any time a teacher tosses the chalk up and down in their hand, you know you're in trouble, because they think they're so cool. The best grade in Mr. Wybold's class was an A triple plus, which no one ever got, quel surprise. But trust me that I was not all alone in my trench of F triple minus.

Cynthia and I are sitting in her living room with her mother and four girls who are younger than us and bigger losers than we ever will be. We had to go around a circle telling one interesting thing about ourselves, and this one girl, Wendy, said, "1961 is the same thing upside down!" First of all, who cares if it is. Secondly, it was supposed to be something interesting about yourself. *What's interesting about me is that I am living in the year 1961, which is the same thing upside down!!!!*

I am wearing the stupid uniform and the stupid beret and the stupid socks and shoes, the whole thing, because I lost the flip of the coin I did with Cynthia. If I'd won, I'd be sitting here in shorts and a blouse like a normal person. My consolation is that the blinds are pulled closed which, according to Mrs. O'Connell, gives the living room a more "woodsy" feel; and that tomorrow night Cynthia and I will be at the party with Bartlett girls; they said I could bring a friend.

We have had our meeting. Now we are talking about the division of labor for when we do our cookout. After that's been decided, we can *finally* change into regular clothes so we can pretend we're in "the dark, dark woods, miles and miles from home." "Yeah, on the planet Mars," I whispered to Cynthia, and she laughed, so we got dagger eyes from her mother, which of course made us laugh more. So far, two jobs have been assigned: making food, and kitchen cleanup. A girl called Maria will be preparing hobo sandwiches, whatever that is, and Wendy will be toasting marshmallows for s'mores over the gas burners of the stove. Maria is a short, dark-haired girl with huge brown eyes, who looks scared to death. She's so skinny her uniform hangs off her. But she is so fired up about Girl Scouts she's wearing the official scarf tied around her neck, and she brought along the official Girl Scout knapsack, which caused Mrs. O'Connell to nearly have a heart attack of joy, and she had to stand up and show everyone what a wonderful thing it was. Wendy is the opposite. Huge. She has a laugh like a bark and everything is funny to her: "Hi, my name is Wendy, *Ha ha ha!!!* She has her blond hair in ponytails with ribbons on them, and at the end of the ribbons are little fuzzy pins that are bugs. Do not ask me.

The two other girls are twins named Mandy and Elaine, both with frizzy red hair and terrible posture. They smile and whisper to one another even though Mrs. O'Connell has said pointedly that we must all remember the golden rule of groups: No one likes to feel left out. But since the meeting, they have not said a word except to each other.

"Now we need to decide who will tell the ghost story," Mrs. O'Connell says. "Hmm, I wonder who-who-whoooooooo would like to do that?" No one says anything. She is trying to be an owl; what are you supposed to say to that.

"Katie?" she says. I knew it. I knew she would ask me to do it. I don't know how, but I knew. I shrug my shoulders. Make a grunting sound.

"Is that a great big Girl Scout yes?" she asks.

I sigh. "Yes, ma'am, I'll tell the ghost story." Here's how it will go: *Once upon a dark and dreary night, a monster named Mrs. O'Connell imprisoned some innocent girls for the purpose of severe torture.*

CYNTHIA!" I WHISPER. "ARE YOU AWAKE?"

"Yes," she whispers back.

It's very late, and everyone is sleeping on the floor pretending they are in the pine needley dirt of the woods. Wendy is sleeping with two teddy bears she brought along—they are married, she told us, and their children are at home lined up on her bed, which is something I might have guessed anyway. Wendy is one of those people you meet and right away you can see into the rest of their lives. How does she take a bath? With bubble gum-smelling stuff in the water. Or Tinkerbell. When she wins at a board game, what does she do? Stands up and claps. Favorite record? "Big Bad John." Underpants? Days of the week that she wears on the actual days. And so on.

Mrs. O'Connell is lying on the sofa, which is her idea of fairness—that way no girl will be jealous of another for getting the prime spot. She is wearing a blue ribbony nightgown with a matching robe, which is not what you would wear. I've been lying awake since we were told no more talking, and I think Cynthia has been too.

"Want to go to your room?" I whisper, and after a moment she says, "Okay."

Very quietly, we make our way upstairs, and when we get to her bedroom, we start laughing. "Don't wake up my dad!" Cynthia says, and I cover my mouth to smother the sounds.

"I can't believe this," I say. "She can't expect that we would ever want to keep doing such stupid things. She's got to understand if we tell her these girls are too young for us. We'll tell her in the morning, after they leave, and we won't take no for an answer."

Cynthia smiles uncertainly, sits down on her bed.

"What? You don't want to keep on, do you?"

She looks up at me, her hands folded in her lap.

"Oh, no. Cynthia, you can't! It's so *awful!*"

"You don't have to come anymore, Katie. But . . ." She shrugs. "She's my dumb mom. And it's my house; I have to be here."

"Well, I'm sorry. I can't do it with you."

"I know," she says. "That's okay."

We hear someone coming down the hall, and there is Cynthia's mother, sticking her head in the door. "Girls?"

"Coming," Cynthia says.

I follow her down the hall, feeling bad for her, like she is one of those French poodle dogs that people put coats and hats on.

WHEN CYNTHIA'S MOTHER drops me off at home, she tries once more to get me to change my mind. "How about if you and Cynthia are coleaders?" she asks, and I say, "Thank you, but it's just not for me. And I'm going to be pretty busy—this new school gave me a lot of reading to do before classes start." Then, before she can say anything else, I open the door and say, "Good luck, though—it seems like you're off to a great start!"

"Katie?"

I turn around. Slowly.

"Don't forget this. Just in case you change your mind." It's the uniform she's handing me, all my things neatly folded in a paper bag.

"Oh," I say. "Well, to be honest—"

"Just take it," she says. "All right? I'd like you to have it."

"Okay," I say, and slam the car door. Not as hard as I'd like to.

She toots the horn as she backs out of the driveway, waves and smiles. I wave back with face A and when I turn around I have on face B.

When I come in the door, I see Ginger sitting at the kitchen table.

"*That* was *awful*," I say.

"Was it?"

She says a normal answer, but it is not a normal tone of voice. "Ginger?" I say, and she says, "Why don't you have a seat here, Katie? Your father will be down in a minute. There's something we need to tell you."

I sit down, my mouth dry. The first thing I think is, Mrs. O'Connell called to complain about the way I behaved last night. Then I think, one of the dogs got hit by a car. But no, I can see that they're both out in the backyard. Then I think, *Diane*.

"What happened?" I say.

"Your dad will be right here. We'd like to tell you together."

"But is it about my sister?"

She shakes her head no, gets up to put her cup in the sink. My father comes into the kitchen, sits at the table, and Ginger stands behind him. Then my father clears his throat and says, "Katie, Mr. Randolph died last night."

I swallow. "Mrs. Randolph, you mean."

"No. It was Mr. Randolph."

I sit still for a long moment. "How do you know?"

"Mrs. Randolph called us. He had a heart attack—went out to get the paper, and didn't come back in. She called the police, and . . . She's in a nursing home. I guess they're going to find her a place near her niece in South Carolina."

"Oh," I say. Inside, some wave of sadness rises up, tall as a wall.

"She said she'd like you to come and see her before she moves," Ginger says. "Would you like to go today? Your father and I will take you."

"Yes. I just . . . I need some time to get ready." I go into my room and close the door and see Mr. Randolph in all his different ways: carefully chopping vegetables, washing his wife's back, listening to me talk like I was saying the most interesting things in the world. Who would have thought that he would die first. It never occurred to me. I sit on the bed and think how life is never safe and they should tell you that right off the bat. Things happen out of order and just plain wrong, and there is not one thing you can do about it. The message of every morning is: ???????????

I put my face into my hands and rock back and forth. No tears. I hope there is a heaven, and I hope Mr. Randolph meets my mother. I hope she invites him into her heavenly living room and together they keep their eyes on all of us down here.

I CAN TELL MY FATHER DISAPPROVES of the house where he drops Cynthia and me off for the party with the Bartlett girls. He says nothing, but his face is hard and bitter. Ginger is quiet too, but it is not anger; it is awe. I feel nervous in the knees to get out of the car, and I don't have much to say myself. The only one who's talking is Cynthia, and she hasn't shut up since we arrived in this neighborhood. "Look at the size of these houses!" she said, and she lives in a pretty big house herself, especially compared to mine. "This is the land of millionaires!"

One of the places we passed had lions at the end of the driveway, and it made me wonder: *What goes through the head of someone who decides to put them there? "I want a thousand rosebushes, a big brass knocker at the door, and oh yes, a couple of lions at the end of the driveway." "Lions, sir?" "Yes, that's right, lions." "Okay, sir."*

"Call us when you're ready to come home," my father says, and I nod.

"This is going to be *fun*," Cynthia says, opening the car door, and I want to tell her to just be quiet, it is not a party for her. Ever since her mother dropped her off at my house tonight, I have been irritated with her. First, she wore something I don't think is right: a dress. I think a skirt and blouse would have been better; a dress seems babyish. Especially with ruffles. And she is so excited, she's talking way louder than usual. Even Ginger noticed this, I saw her smiling to my dad about it on the way over. And now she is rushing out of the car like she knows everyone there, and I want to just take my time, to think about what I'm going to say after I ring the doorbell. But too late, Cynthia rings the doorbell before me, and now the door is opening. There is a tall, blond woman standing there smiling, and behind her is an entryway as big as a gymnasium. She is wearing black pants and a white blouse and gold hoop earrings. "The guest of honor!" she says, stepping aside. I turn around to wave to my father and Ginger, but all I can see is headlights, then the slow backing away of the car, like an animal when it rushes up to something and then changes its mind.

"Welcome, Katie," the woman says warmly, to Cynthia. And Cynthia starts laughing, which is so rude. Then, instead of pointing to me and saying, "That's Katie," she says, "I'm Cynthia O'Connell."

"Glad to meet you, Cynthia," the woman says. "I'm Kay Grasser, Leigh's mother." She doesn't look like a real mother. She is the Donna Reed type of mother, with no gravy stains on the apron. "How nice of you to come along."

Well, I guess I'll just go sit on the curb and wait for Cynthia to come out from the party. Make some grass harps and wave at the cars that go by. This edgy meanness is growing and growing inside me; I don't know what to do to stop it.

But then Mrs. Grasser turns to me and says, "And *you* must be *Katie.*"

"Yes, ma'am."

"Come in," she says, "Everyone is here; they're all downstairs." She leads us down a long hall to a door that goes into the basement. This is not a basement like we have, with the washer and dryer and old wooden table to fold clothes on, with storage boxes lined up along the walls and a bare bulb hanging from the ceiling that you turn on by pulling a string, with a smell of bleach mixed with damp earth. No. This doesn't look like a basement at all. For one thing, there is wood on the walls. For another, there is a bar. A real bar, with a mirror and tall stools and a million glasses lined up on shelves. I see a girl standing behind the bar, pouring a Coke into a glass for another girl sitting on one of the stools. On a low coffee table there are two pizzas, but no one has eaten any yet. In the corner there are three more girls, standing around the stereo, looking through a stack of albums. They are all wearing skirts and blouses, so I was right. One girl has on a sweater like the one I want—black, with ribbing. And she gets to wear it even though school hasn't started. Another is wearing a wraparound skirt, something I also want but doubt that I'll get. This is something I cannot get Ginger to understand, that you cannot go to Wards to get fashionable clothes, that regular loafers are not Weejuns.

"Leigh?" Mrs. Grasser says, "Here are Katie and her friend, Cynthia."

"Hi, Katie!" Leigh says, looking at Cynthia.

Again! "*I'm* Katie," I say, and go over and hold out my hand. Leigh hesitates just the slightest bit, and I realize I've made a mistake offering to shake hands. But she's being nice about it. She shakes my hand and then goes so far as to shake Cynthia's too. Cynthia starts giggling, and I want to say, *Don't!* but instead I just stare straight ahead to show that I am my own separate self. Leigh says, "We're really glad you're coming to Bartlett. Let me introduce you to the other girls."

Everyone comes over to make a perfumey circle around me, and I can't believe it. Pretty girls in nice clothes who know how to do things are smiling at me and saying how much I'll like their school. One, Caitlin, has suspiciously streaky blond hair and I remember what Cherylanne said about dyed hair. But she is being so nice, everyone is. I am in the basement of such a fancy house at a party given in honor of me. And this is all because of Mr. Randolph, who has died before I could tell him anything about it.

I think of how Mrs. Randolph looked in the nursing home,

bewildered and sad, how mostly she just patted my arm and thanked me and said how much her husband liked me. How he was wonderful to the end, wasn't he? And then she just looked out the window for a time before she turned back to me. Her eyes had lost the light they usually had; they were a flat and vacant blue. I said I would come and see her one more time before she left—her niece will be there to drive her to South Carolina on Wednesday. "I'll look forward to that, Katie," she said, and then it seemed like all she wanted to do was rest. I left her lying in the hospital bed, holding her purse on her lap like it was Mr. Randolph's hand.

So there she is at the end of her life which is closing down, and here I am at the beginning of mine, which is opening up. Cynthia asks if I want to go and get some pizza, and I tell her no, but go ahead, like it is my house, like everything here is mine. It kind of feels that way. It feels like some part of me that was curled down and waiting in the dark has risen, and now stands stretching and strong in the sunshine. *I knew it.*

ONCE I SAW THE DOGS get into a tug-of-war over a dish-cloth that had fallen off the clothesline. They stood facing each other, their paws firmly planted, growling and giving a shake every so often, each unwilling to let go. This is how it feels inside me now. I am lying in bed wide awake, so thrilled to know that I will be part of the group I just met, but there is another feeling in me as well, and that is shame. Each feeling wants to win.

About halfway through the party, Leigh called me into the little bathroom in the basement. She said it was so I could try on some of her lip gloss that I had admired, but that wasn't it. What she wanted was to talk about Cynthia. She closed the door, sat on the closed seat of the toilet, and said, "This Cynthia. Is she a good friend of yours?"

I knew why she was asking. Cynthia was acting like an idiot. She was just too excited, talking loud, laughing like a braying donkey, telling jokes that were not funny, even a really stupid riddle, once: "Why did Tigger look in the toilet? He was trying to find Pooh." I thought about answering Leigh by saying I knew Cynthia was weird, but also she was pretty nice, you could tell her anything, part of her problem was she had to live with a crazy mother, things like that. But when I opened my mouth, all that came out was, "Not really. She's just someone I go to school with. I kind of had to bring her."

Leigh nodded, like she was an old, wise person. And then she said, "Well, good. Because we're all going shopping tomorrow, and I wanted to invite you, but not if . . ."

"Oh, no," I said, quickly. "She doesn't have to come." And then, to prove how much I understood that Cynthia was not part of us, I told Leigh about the Girl Scout thing.

"Are you *kidding?*" Leigh kept saying, louder and louder, and I kept saying, *No!* Leigh was listening so carefully to me, as though we were sudden best friends, and I had this feeling of joy like I just got rescued. I remembered a time in school last year when I saw two very popular girls go into a bathroom stall together. They were giggling and talking low so no one could hear. I looked at their shoes, at their purses on the floor. I went into the stall next to them and sat on the toilet with my hands on my lap, trying to hear. But it wouldn't matter if I did, I still would never have anything to do with girls like that. Now, suddenly, I was in one of those crowds. I wanted to keep going, I wanted Leigh to be more and more interested in me, and so I tried to make the story of Cynthia better and better. I told about how the first time I went to her house, she showed me how she could fart from her vagina. That was a good one; Leigh's mouth opened wide, and then she took my arm and squeezed it tight, and began laughing and gasping, her eyes wide. I felt a delicious power, like how you feel when you're holding the platter up high and everyone is clamoring around you. I laughed too, when I told the story, remembering Cynthia lying on the floor with her legs in the air and that triumphant look on her face; but also I laughed because it felt so good to know I had finally arrived at a place where I had been longing to be. I thought I could say to Leigh, "Can I borrow your bracelet?" and she would say, "Of course!" and unclasp it, and when I put it on, the metal would still be warm from her skin. I saw that I would have some golden protection that comes from being in a circle of girls like this; the things that used to hurt me wouldn't anymore. I was all of a sudden a Bartlett girl.

When we came out of the bathroom, there was a terrible shock. Because standing there was Cynthia, her face so still and straight. At first I tried to act like nothing happened, but it didn't work—she had heard everything. She looked at me and she didn't say anything, but in her eyes were a million things coming out in a sorrowful beam directed straight at me. I felt a blush start to creep up my neck.

"Cynthia!" Leigh said. "Are you having a good time?"

"I want to go home."

Leigh looked at me quickly, a little smile on her face.

"Cynthia," I said, but she ignored me, just asked Leigh, "Can I please use a phone?"

"Sure," Leigh said, shrugging. "Come on upstairs with me."

Cynthia followed her up the basement steps, her back straight, her purse tucked under her arm. I knew everything that was in that purse. I'd written notes to Cynthia in school that she kept in the zippered compartment in the middle. I'd opened her makeup case many times to use her comb or mirror, and I'd helped her pick out the wallet she carried, a blue plastic one with a picture of Troy Donahue she'd cut out of a movie magazine and put in the first picture holder. I'd taken money she'd offered me from that wallet when I didn't have enough.

I knew where Cynthia would put her purse when she got home, and I knew what her room would look like after she went to bed, how she'd have the little night light on because she was afraid of the dark. I felt a giant fist begin to squeeze my stomach, a sense of profound regret that made me want to do something to erase all that had happened.

But I did not call Cynthia's name, or follow her up the stairs, or even pay attention to what my insides were trying to tell me. Instead, I turned back to that circle of girls gathered now around the pizza, each bright and brilliant as a gemstone to me, each as desirable. I took in a breath, put a smile on my face, and went over to stand among them.

Now I turn onto my side and finger the charms on the bracelet that Leigh really did lend me. At the time, the bracelet seemed so much, a trophy. Now it is just a bracelet with charms that dig into my skin, hurting me, and I take it off and put it by the side of the bed.

In one night, a new life has started. I feel bad about Cynthia, but I would feel bad even if she hadn't caught me talking about her. I guess it always hurts to move away from something, even if it's not another city you're going to, but another way of being.

THE NEXT MORNING I AM in the middle of a dream when I hear Ginger's voice calling me, telling me there's a phone call for me. I am instantly awake, excited, remembering last night and thinking—hoping—it's Leigh. But then I realize it's probably only Cynthia, healed from last night's humiliation, calling to ask what are we going to do today. And I'll have to tell her nothing. I'll be as gentle as I can.

But it is not Cynthia, it is Mr. Wexler, asking if I can baby-sit tonight. I am so surprised to hear from him—I'd thought we were all done. But Mrs. Wexler has come back, they are going out for a night on the town, and I will earn a lot of money because they will be out really late. There are a million questions I want to ask him: Is she sorry? Are you happy? What did the kids say? Where *was* she? But of course I don't ask those questions, I act like nothing at all is unusual, and I agree to be there at seven o'clock. I am actually looking forward to seeing the boys. Well, Henry, anyway.

I go out into the kitchen and smell Ginger's French toast. There is a stack of it, already done, sitting on my favorite blue plate on the kitchen counter. She makes it for special occasions. I guess she's happy about my new friends—she got excited last night when she and my father came to pick me up and I told them I had been invited to go shopping with Leigh and some of the other girls. She looked at my father like, *Isn't she something?* but my father didn't do anything back. When I'd told him Cynthia had gone home early, he'd said, "Is that right," and then he hadn't talked anymore.

I look at the clock; thirteen after eleven. I believe this is the latest I've ever slept, and a sure sign that I really am a teenager now; they always sleep late. I sit at the table with my breakfast and try to remember every nice thing that was said to me at the party last night. It's no use, though, because Ginger is vacuuming my bedroom, and that vacuum is so loud it seems like it sucks all your thoughts up with the dirt. The vacuum cuts out suddenly, and I hear a little cry from Ginger. Then it is quiet.

I get up and run to my room, wishing my father were home, thinking Ginger must have hurt herself. But it isn't that. Instead, Ginger is sitting on the floor, the vacuum turned on its side, and she is looking up into it. She sees me and says, "Katie, did you have something on the floor by your bed?"

I start to say no, but then I remember. I feel as though the French toast I just ate has turned into bricks.

I sit on the floor beside Ginger. "It was a bracelet. I put it there last night."

Ginger looks at me, and I know what she's thinking. *Well, you can say good-bye to that.*

"It belongs to the girl that had the party," I say, "the one I'm going shopping with today. Leigh." It is so strange to me how in the middle of an emergency, out pops a kind of brag. This is how it looks in my brain:

SHOPPING WITH LEIGH!!!!! (broken bracelet) SHOPPING WITH LEIGH!!!!!!

Ginger sets her mouth in a firm line. "We'll get it." She opens the bottom of the vacuum and starts pulling things out. Dog hair, dirt, and then a charm. Then another, and then part of the chain. I think of handing the pieces of bracelet back to Leigh, how her face will look, and how she will be thinking, *I never should have let her borrow it. I should have known what kind of person she is. She's out.*

"Maybe we can get it fixed," Ginger says, but then she pulls another charm out that is all twisted. "Or buy another one," she says, quietly.

"I don't have any idea where she got it," I say, sadly. I sit back on my heels, sigh. I wish I had gotten out of bed to put the bracelet on my desk; I was pure lazy. But then I get an idea. I tell Ginger, "Maybe I can just call her and tell her I like it so much I want one, too. And we can quick go get one before she comes to pick me up."

Ginger nods. "It's worth a try."

Leigh and her mother are coming at one; I need to call quickly. I go out into the hall to look up her number in the phone book. When the phone rings, Leigh answers. "Hi," I say, "it's Katie."

"Oh, hi!" she says, and when I heard the warmth in her voice I feel happy all over again to be in the circle, even though I have destroyed the first thing she lent me. "Are you still coming?" she asks.

"Yes," I say, "but I was just sitting here with my stepmother, and we were talking about your bracelet, and we wondered where you got it—I'd like to get one, too."

"Oh, my grandmother sent me that. She and my grandfather own a jewelry store in Arizona."

"Oh," I say. I am sunk.

"But you can have it," she says. "Just keep it."

"Oh, no."

"I hardly ever wear it. Really."

"Well, okay if you're sure." If my heart was a body, it would be turning cartwheels.

"I have to go, now," Leigh says. "Kristi just got here. So we'll see you at one?"

"Yes," I say. "At one."

I wonder what they'll wear. I need to go and look in my closet and try some things out. This could take a while. When you get in a group like this, you have to start doing things right.

153

IT IS NINE-THIRTY, and there's nothing good on the channel that comes in well at the Wexlers'. I am sitting on the sofa, thinking about the last time I was here, and Cynthia and I looked at a movie magazine. Maybe I'll call her to come over. I'm so bored I actually did some cleaning here—dusted the living room, swept the kitchen floor, scoured the bathroom sink.

I go into the kitchen and dial Cynthia's number. She picks up on the first ring. "Cynthia!" I say. "It's me, Katie." There is silence, then a gentle click, then a dial tone. Well, what is wrong with this phone?

I dial again, and this time Cynthia's mother picks up. "Hi," I say. "It's Katie. I just got disconnected from Cynthia. Can you put her back on?"

"She's not here."

"Pardon?"

"She is not here. She went out with some friends."

Ho. This is a pretty good joke, since Cynthia's "friends" consist of me. "Well," I say. "When she comes back, will you ask her to call me at the Wexlers'? I'll give you the number."

"I don't need the number," Mrs. O'Connell says.

"You have it?" I say. I wonder why she has it.

"I don't need it. *Cynthia* doesn't need it. She won't be calling you again, Katie."

Everything stops. Even my breathing. Sitting here alone in this kitchen, I feel as though a million eyes are suddenly on me. I can't think of anything to say, and the silence takes on a terrible weight.

Finally, I clear my throat and start to ask how long Cynthia will be "gone," but Mrs. O'Connell interrupts me. "I think that's all we have to say to you," she says, and I think, *Oh, Cynthia. Don't let your mother talk for you.* But I don't say that, I just say, "Oh, okay," and hang up the phone. I sit still, my hands folded for a long time, thinking. And then, I can't help it, I dial Cynthia's number again.

"Hello?"

Mrs. O'Connell again.

"It's Katie," I say. "I know what you just said, but can I please speak to Cynthia? I know she's there; she just answered the phone. Could you just let me talk to her?"

"She doesn't want to talk to you."

I laugh a little, but quietly. Mrs. O'Connell doesn't know. What does she know about me and Cynthia? Nothing. "I know she's kind of mad at me, but I just need to explain something to her. Could you please tell her I'm on the phone and that . . . Could you just ask her if she'd come and talk to me?"

A long moment. And then, "Yes. I will ask her, Katie. But I don't think she will want to come to the phone, and frankly, I don't blame her."

So Cynthia told her mother what happened. Oh, I wish she hadn't told her. At the other end of the phone line, I hear Mrs. O'Connell breathing. Well, what does she want? Finally, I just say, "I'll just wait and see," and then the phone gets put down. In the distance, I hear, "Cynthia! It's Katie, *again.* Do you want to talk to her?" There is a long pause. And then I hear the phone being picked up. Thank goodness. Now I can tell Cynthia why I did what I did, that it was nothing against her, really, we can still be friends, she and I will just be in a different group, this is what I have decided. It was wrong to think that I would no longer have her as a friend. I care about her, there is a place to put her. She can come over tonight and we can talk some more and get ourselves right again. But it is not Cynthia on the phone. It is her mother, Mrs. Icicle, saying "Well, it's just as I told you, Katie. She doesn't want to talk to you. Please don't call anymore, now."

I can feel something in my throat growing larger, and it makes my voice not quite itself when I say, "Well, could you just tell her one thing?"

Mrs. O'Connell sighs.

"Will you just tell her to call me when she's ready?"

"Yes." She says it so quickly, I know she won't do it.

"Thank you," I say, and Mrs. O'Connell hangs up. No You're welcome, no good-bye, no nothing. I wonder where she will go now. Will she go into Cynthia's room and rub her back, which I happen to know Cynthia doesn't even like? Will she pop popcorn for them to eat together while they watch TV? Will they talk about me? Is it my turn now to be the one outside the door? It feels terrible to think about, even if it's only Mrs. O'Connell gossiping about you, and who cares what she thinks.

I sit for a while staring at the kitchen window over the sink. It is a square of blackness, now. When I got here, I could look out and see birds, see flowers, see kids playing hopscotch. Now there is just the sight of my own dumb face, reflected back.

I go upstairs to look in at Mark and David. They are sound asleep; there is a smell in the air of it. Then I go into Henry's room. I watch him sleeping for a while, then whisper his name. Nothing. I go to stand beside his bed, call him again. Still nothing. I shake his shoulder, and he frowns, then opens his eyes. He looks strange without his glasses, like a newborn bird without feathers. "What," he says, his voice thick with sleep.

"Want to come downstairs?" I ask.

"What for?" He's a little crabby.

"You can watch TV with me, or we can play a game, just you and me. We won't tell your brothers, it'll be just you and me."

He closes his eyes again.

"Henry?"

"What?" His eyes still closed.

"Want to come down with me? Want to stay up late?"

He turns away from me, resettles on his side. "I'm *tired*. Stop waking me *up*."

"Okay," I say. "Sorry."

I head downstairs, stop at the landing, and stare at the empty living room. The sofa and the chairs seem to have turned around to stare back at me. I will now have to sit for about six thousand hours doing nothing. And I can't talk to Cynthia. I feel like someone has abruptly removed a coat I didn't know I had on.

I turn on the television again, but it is only a boring talk show host, fake smiling and slapping his knee like the joke is so funny, but mainly his eyeballs look to see: Is the camera on him?

I get up and head for the junk drawer of the kitchen to find some scrap paper. I will write a poem about a bare bulb in a room without furniture. This poem will belong to me, and I will not be sharing it with anyone. I stare at the paper, stare at the paper, then put the pencil down.

If Cynthia had just come over, I would have apologized so truly. And then I would have told her about this afternoon, about all the mistakes I made. How I got dressed up to go to the mall, even tied a scarf around my neck trying to look French, and sprayed myself with Intimate perfume, and wore nylons and a new pair of flats that Ginger just got me for school, when the rest of the girls wore jeans and blouses, loafers with socks. I would have told her how when we had lunch, I got the worst seat, the most outside one, and that I dripped ketchup on my blouse and the girls made eyes at each other that they thought I didn't see, but I did. I would have told her that they asked a lot about my writing—they knew it was because of

that that I got admitted into their school. They even asked me to
tell one of my poems, and I did, I recited the one called "Love,"
where the wave comes up onto the sand and takes away only a few
grains of sand from all that is available to it. I wanted so much for
them to like it. But when I was through, they just looked at me like,
"What?" and I had to try to explain it to them, which did not come
out so well. It was not like when Cynthia read it and then looked
up at me all thoughtful and said, "And yet if it took too much sand,
it wouldn't be water anymore."

Sitting here in the quiet, I feel like I have come to the end of a
dead-end road. I have to face up to the fact that the reason the
Bartlett girls are interested in me is that they want me to help them
write the papers we have to turn in about the books we have to read
this summer. That's all. It is not because of my sparkling personality
and winning ways. It is not that I have suddenly become one of
them. Leigh wants me to write a poem about her and her boyfriend,
too, and when I told her I would do it, I felt robbed.

I would have told Cynthia about how one time I lagged way
behind them as we walked, just to see if they would notice, and
they did not. How in the car on the way back they talked about
people and things I knew nothing about, until their mother said,
"How about including Katie in the conversation?" which was even
worse. Cynthia would have said something good after I told her all
that. Something funny. And some part of myself that felt like it had
fallen off the shelf would have been put back up again. As it turns
out, it is just me alone, thinking, How do I fix everything? and
coming up with nothing.

I wish for the first time in my life that I was a boy. I don't think
things work for them in the same way as girls; they have thicker
skin. If I were a boy and Cynthia were a boy, she wouldn't have told
her mother about what happened. She wouldn't have said anything; she would have just gone to bed. Probably without washing
her face. And then the next day I could have gone over and just

socked her on the arm and she could have said cut it out, dickhead, and things would have been back to normal, just like that. We would go out and do some rough things and then power ride our bikes over to McDonald's, get about forty-five cheeseburgers apiece, and have a belching contest. Then we could sit on the curb not talking, just knowing we were locked into our friendship no matter what. And that night we'd go behind a garage and smoke, toss the lit butts up in the air to make an arc of light before they landed. Not think about girls or how to impress them, because they did all the worrying for us. Yes. At this moment, I wish I were a boy named Jack Armstrong who did not just mess up his only good friendship for the sake of a bunch of phonies.

IT'S LATE AFTERNOON, and I am out in one of the fields that surround this community of houses where I live. It's so hard to think that these fields exist when, day after day, you walk down a sidewalk past house after house after house. But go far enough out and you see how it was before everything started. Which I believe is true of all things.

It's beautiful outside, the kind of day where the sun touches you like mothers touch their babies' cheeks. Your breath rides in your chest like a slow-swaying hammock, and your eyes see in the rich way: Yellow isn't yellow, it's butterscotch; the red on the roses is velvet. On days like this, you wish everything would slow down; you wish time could just stop for a while. But of course that never happens. When a good thing comes along, time is like a flirty girl lifting her skirt and running away, laughing over her shoulder at you. But let the dentist at that cavity way in the back of your mouth, and you will see how time can work the other way.

In my pocket is a letter from Cherylanne. I told her about what happened with Cynthia, and, judging from the thickness of the envelope, she has a lot of advice to give me. Now that I am alone and sure that no one can interrupt me, I will read it.

Dear Katie,

Well, it is the job of a friend to a friend to speak the truth and so I am going to tell you yes, you are right you have screwed up royally. You have to follow certain rules when you are talking about somebody, and the most important of course is MAKE SURE THE PERSON IS NOT THERE. Or you will have to bear the consequences. Which now you know all about.

One thing I want to tell you is not to feel bad that you felt the urge to gossip because it is a basic need like cereal. It is not nice, but we all like to do it. Except saints, who nobody can stand to be around. It will not do any good for me to tell you the obvious such as you never should have invited Cynthia to a party with girls like that, to speak frankly but I hope it doesn't hurt your feelings, you would not have been invited either except that you got in their school and probably they have to have welcome parties which their moms make them do. I have heard about that. Not to hurt your feelings. But anyway, once she was invited probably you should have explained some things not to do, and for sure you should never have talked so loud behind a closed door when it was every possibility someone could listen, especially the disaster person, Cynthia herself. But again, there is no sense in going on about the past is the past.

So now what you have to do in my opinion is a very hard thing, which is you have to do nothing. That is so you can wait for the balm of time to do its magic, time really does heal all wounds. Most of them. So, just do other things and do NOT call her again as her mother might answer for one thing and there is nothing she would like better than to make you feel bad because you made her daughter feel bad. This is how mothers are, which I know a lot more about now that the hormones of motherhood are racing through me like Andy Granatelli. I have feelings like I never had before and it is all on account of the baby growing inside. I don't even care how Darren has become some-what cold, at least he is going to do right by me. After a while, he will get used to being married and my goal besides having a healthy baby is to make sure Darren ends up having a spring in his step as he comes up the walk to our home. And I will do that, you know how when I get determined, I can do anything.

But we are talking about you, right. So Katie you must trust that if you had a good friendship the rags of it will come together and mend into a new garment. It will not be exactly like before of course, because you have done a hateful thing. Which sort of you couldn't help it, it was the intense peer pressure of adoles-cence (remember how I used to tell you about that?). You could try praying, although so far that has not always worked out for me, but many others swear by it.

I wish we weren't so far apart now and I could invite you over to have a glass of limeade at the kitchen table and we could talk both at the same time instead of I write a letter, you write a letter, and then about a thousand years go by and then we write again. But even if that is so, just know that I am here in my heart for you because we used to be good friends and that always stays and that is what you will come to see about Cynthia, she will come around like an old cat.

I guess that's it for now, and to summarize, just remember: do nothing for now. Just wait.

Bubba is in heaven because he was in the newspaper for foot-ball and now he is even worse to live with. It is only the paper they give away at the supermarket, but Bubba's fat face was right on page one and now he sits around on the front porch like he is waiting for Hollywood to drive by and say at last we've found our leading man forever. He did try to do one nice thing, believe it or not. He came in my room the other night when I was a little bit crying which is not unusual for someone in my position. And he sat on my bed with his stupid football in his lap and he said, "I'll bet your baby turns out to be good looking because look at us. And it could have my genes for sports talent, too. Probably it will if it's a boy." I said thanks Bubba, and he said you're welcome and then he stood around for a while like an elephant in a china shop and then he made some grunt and said, "See you," and left. I'm telling you I had to smile after he closed the door so soft and caretaking.

My parents are fine, and if my mother could advise you about your problem I know just what she would say, don't you? "Well, sweetheart, there's no point in crying over spilt milk, you might as well get right back up on the horse that bit you." Followed up by a kiss and a hug. And then of course she would feed you which we hate to admit it but it almost always does feel good to eat something someone has fixed for us when we are hurting. (P.S. My mother has given me her chili recipe which as you know was always TOP SECRET. Because I am going to be married and I'll need it. Believe it or not, one of the secret ingredients is orange juice!!!!)

I have a little pot belly now which as you know I would never ever have had otherwise. It is offset by how my hair and nails are growing. And I probably glow, although it is a bit hard for me to see it, even though Lord knows I have tried in every kind of light. But others have said it's so. Soon all I will wear is maternity clothes, which believe me, they are not the height of fashion.

Well, I guess this letter is long enough! I will try to write again soon, but the best intentions are of mice and men, as you know. Here comes some love to you, Katie, and a comforting and resounding pat on the back. Close your eyes and you can feel it.

Your friend forever,
Cherylanne

(and her baby girl Sandra or Annette or Scarlet and if it's a boy?????? as there are no good boy names, including Darren)

I fold the letter up, put it back in my pocket. Cherylanne and I are a lot alike right now. We have both blundered into a place where we'd rather not be, and now we have to make the best of it. I lie down on the warm dirt, which smells so calm, and look up into the sky. It seems like people are all the time making themselves themselves, but they don't really know it. You can only have true vision when you look behind. A person can slide so fast into being something they never really intended. I wonder if you can truly resurrect your own self.

In an hour or so, my father will be home for dinner, and I am going to talk to him about how I don't want to go to the Bartlett School after all. I will keep Cherylanne's letter in my pocket to help me when I say it. The thing about people like Cherylanne is, you can't be so fast about what to think of them. It's like the way you find beautiful crystals inside some plain gray rocks—who would have known they were there? Cherylanne says a lot of strange things, and her style is not exactly Shakespeare, but this is the first time I have felt soothed inside since I did what I did. And it is Cherylanne who did that. I also feel some hope about the future. Which will not include the Bartlett girls, I hope.

This morning, Leigh called to see if her poem about her and her boyfriend was ready, and I said not yet. Then there was a moment of cool silence, as though I had offended her. I suppose she thought I should be honored to write about her and Barrett, but I don't even know him. And even if I did, I don't want to write about what someone else tells me to write about.

When I start a poem, the center of me lifts up—I feel myself floating before I start to put the words down. Sometimes they are good words and sometimes they're not, but always the lift comes to take me to the place that is not really a place, yet feels realer than this ground I lie on. But when someone tells me what to write a poem about, I'm not lifted at all, I'm weighed down. It's as though something comes down over me, cutting off my view, taking up my breathing space. I can't do it. And I don't want to do it. And I *won't* do it for Leigh; this is what comes to me now. I won't do it because I don't have to do it. In the dirt, I use a stick to write *no*. Then I stand up and start back home.

G UESS WHO CALLED?" Ginger says, when I walk in the door.

"Cynthia?" I ask quickly, and Ginger gets a soft look and says, "No. Not yet." I told Ginger about what happened, although I must admit I made myself look better than I actually was. I said that Leigh was talking about Cynthia and that I didn't defend her, and that's all. This was a lie of omission, of course, which, according to Father Compton, is just as bad as other lies, but I just couldn't tell the whole truth right then. Later I will. It will have to be at the right time.

But now Ginger says, "It was Mrs. Randolph. She'll be leaving tomorrow afternoon, and she said she would love to see you before she goes."

"Oh," I say. "Okay." Mrs. Randolph wants to see the me from before. But I am different now, I am someone who did a bad thing, and who now wants to refuse the gift that her husband gave me. I won't tell her I don't want to go to the Bartlett school anymore. But I wonder if it will leak out my eyes. I wonder if I'll end up telling her and then she'll feel so disappointed in me too.

"I can run you over to the nursing home tomorrow morning," Ginger says. "But it will have to be before ten."

"Okay," I say. "That's fine."

Now I hear the car door slam, and here comes my father up the steps. I swallow hard, and go to wash my hands before I take my place at the table. Sometimes I wish people didn't have to wash so much. Sometimes when you've been outside and gotten dirt on your hands, it just feels so friendly and connected.

MACARONI AND CHEESE IS WHAT Ginger has made, with little baby peas to go along with it, which is the perfect choice. Fruit salad with whipped cream for dessert, and the only thing wrong is that she uses oranges in it, the cheater fruit. My father is sitting in his army uniform with the neck of the shirt open, and you can see his T-shirt which is so white it's almost blue. He is not saying anything, which is normal. Ginger is making a little comment here and there, also normal. She says things in a low and musical voice that always reminds me of the sound birds make when they're settling down for the night.

Well, here goes.

"Dad?"

He looks at me.

"I was thinking about the Bartlett school."

Nothing.

"I was thinking I might not go."

He smiles and nods his head in a knowing way. "Oh, you'll go, all right." He looks at Ginger, who smiles back at him, *Yes indeed*. They think I'm just nervous.

"But the thing is, I might not *want* to go."

His blue eyes on me. "What do you mean?"

"Well, I've decided something. I've decided my regular school will be all right. It will be fine. I want to go to my regular school, it's really pretty much the same as the Bartlett school."

"Your regular school is nothing like the Bartlett school. You are very lucky to have gotten a scholarship, and you'll go there."

His voice has risen and everything else has gotten so still. This is the part where I am supposed to put my head down. *Okay. Sorry.*

But I don't. I put down my fork and look right at him. "Dad. I have changed my mind. I have come to know some of the girls and I don't think I'd fit in. I don't think I'd be happy there."

"Well, I'll tell you what. You can be *happy* when you come home."

"Honey?" Ginger says. "What happened? Why in the world would you want to turn down an opportunity like this?"

"I just don't like the kids. I don't think I—"

"You're going," my father says. "End of discussion. Pass me the bread, Ginger."

I wonder how it feels to say this, to have that kind of power. I wonder, Does it feel like a thrill, do your insides swell up proud like a peacock on full display? I wonder when it started, my father being mean. When did he go from being a kid himself to saying *Do it! Now!* with veins of his neck standing out.

Sometimes I try to remember things my mother told me about the awful way he was raised. But why does he have to keep on going. Why would you take something bad out of your mouth and then hand it to another, saying, Here. Eat this.

I look at Ginger, *Help me,* but she says nothing. She agrees with him. She doesn't know what's happened, that I am not by any means a member of the Bartlett School Girls' Club, and I never will be. I am in the club with Cynthia, only now she won't be with me in anything, not anymore. What do I have left, I wonder.

I sit and stare at my father, but he won't look at me. I don't know what to say to make him hear. I see the muscles in his jaws moving as he chews. He takes a long drink of water. *Dinner,* that's what's in his head. That person inside me who rose up so confident when I was out in the field this afternoon is not inside me anymore. Nothing is inside me anymore. Wind could rush through.

I look at the kitchen clock and wish it moved in years instead of hours. Because I'm going to California to live near my sister, Diane, as soon as I'm done with high school. You think everything can change, but the truth is that some things never can. Living with him is like living in a box. Ginger can hang curtains and put some pictures on the wall, but it is always a box. You can't move far. You can only rise up when you're able and move out altogether.

"Finish your dinner," he tells me, and I pick up my fork, swallow around the lump.

I won't write him, either. I won't call. *Huh*, he will say, sitting out on the back steps at night, his cigarette held low between his knees. He will run a hand over the top of his crew cut, stare at the clothesline pole standing simple under the stars, and he will say it again: *Huh*. Ginger, sitting beside him, will say nothing, but he will hear exactly what she is thinking. That he will hear.

I AM IN MY ROOM, SITTING AT MY DESK. Right after dinner, Leigh called to say she and Barrett were going out tomorrow night, it was his birthday, and could I read that poem over the phone to her so she could put in her own writing and give it to him for one of his presents? And oh yes, did I want to come with her and Kristi to a movie . . . sometime? Right.

But. I have to go to the Bartlett school and I will have to be around those girls. Every day, I will have to be around them. Look where I have gotten myself. I lay out a piece of paper, smooth it with my hand. Then I pick up a pencil and smell it for the mix of lead and wood. I take in a long breath, stare at the page. And then I put the pencil down and go out to the hall phone to call Cynthia. My father and Ginger went to a movie; at last I have some privacy.

"Hello?" Mrs. O'Connell says. I say nothing. "Hello?" she says, again, and waits for a moment, then hangs up. I go back to my room and sit at my desk. Here is what I am: a sandbag in a chair.

I pick up the pencil. It is a little log, heavy in my hand, and that is all. I turn off my desk lamp, lean back in my chair. Outside, branches move in the wind. It's supposed to rain later. My inside self and my outside self used to match. A compass needle pointed true north. Now the needle spins around and around, indicating the sad direction of nowhere.

I get up to turn on the radio, then turn it off. I stand at the window, looking out at the house across the street. Someone is in a kitchen in her robe, eating something from a bowl. Some people are watching television. Some houses are all dark, the people gone. Someone has the lawn sprinkler on, and the high fan of water moves back and forth, back and forth.

I think for a while, then go to my desk and write a few lines. I read them out loud to myself in a whisper. Again. Then I cross out one line and substitute another, read that aloud. Good enough.

I go to the phone and call Leigh. She answers on the first ring. "It's me, Katie," I say. "I have your poem."

"Already?" she says. "Wow, you're a genius."

"Do you have a pen?"

"Hold on." I wait for a moment, and she comes back, breathless. "He is going to be so surprised! He will never believe that I wrote a poem for him!"

I say nothing, waiting for her to realize her error. But she doesn't.

"It's a haiku," I tell her.

"Oh?"

"That's what I like doing, lately." An inside blush of shame, *Sorry*.

"Well, I *guess* that's all right. So how does it go?"

I hold up the paper, recite the words I've written to her:

> *Love alights inside*
> *On glad heart's branch of welcome*
> *Wings flutter, then still*

"Wait," she says, and my stomach takes a ride to the basement. " 'On glad heart's branch of welcome?' " She says the phrase like she is holding it away from herself with two fingers.

"Yes."

"I don't get it."

"Well, it's . . . It's like you are waiting for love? And your heart extends itself? So love has a place to land? And it's glad when it does?"

"I see."

No, she doesn't.

"Um . . ."

"If you don't like it," I say, "maybe you could just find something else in a poetry book and copy that out."

"Yeah," she says, doubtfully. Irritably. "I suppose. But I guess I was—well, it's really good what you did! But I was sort of hoping for something more personal. Where somebody could read it and know the poem was about *us*. Like, his eye color and mine could be in there, something like that. Or how we met."

"How did you meet?"

"At a school dance. It was so great."

"Well," I say. "Here's my idea for you. *You* write it."

A moment of silence. And then, "Oh, okay. Now you've gone and got your feelings all hurt."

"Not at all."

"I'm sorry. I know people who try to write poetry are oversensitive."

"No, I just think you should write it. You know what you want. You can do it. I can tell by the way you're coming up with ideas already."

A moment of silence. And then, "Really? Do you really think so?" I can practically hear her smile.

"Sure."

"Well . . . what rhymes with green that could be in a love poem? Because his eyes are green. Maybe . . . bean?"

"Or dream," I say.

"That's it! It *was* like a dream! And I felt like a queen, I could use *'queen'*!"

"There you go," I say. "I have to hang up now. Good luck, and I'm sure he'll like it."

173

"Thanks, Kate!"

Kate. I have never been called that in my life. I start to say you're welcome, but then don't. I put the phone back in its cradle, so gently. Just to see if I can do it without making a sound. Like no wake in the water. No evidence of anything.

Back in my room, I stand at the window again for a long time. It's dark out, but the full moon is bright enough that you can see a little circle of leaves skittering down the street. I turn them into Greek women holding hands and dancing barefoot around and around. Thin ribbons woven into their long, black hair. But the image won't hold, it fades, and I see again only leaves, curled up at the edges and dying. I don't know where they came from. It's summer; nothing should be dying so soon.

I go into the basement. Maybe I'll do a load of towels and surprise Ginger. Fold them square and even. Let the good deed make up for the bad ones. I open my mouth to let out a low moan but it gets louder and louder like it is its own self. Finally, I just sit on a pile of dirty laundry and let the song of grief sing itself out.

GINGER DROPS ME OFF IN FRONT of the nursing home where Mrs. Randolph is staying. "Will half an hour be all right?" she says, and I say yes, a little worried that it will be too long.

When I come into the hallway, I can't see at first because of the contrast: so sunny outside, so dark and cool inside. But then my eyes adjust and I see the desk where the nurses are, and a woman sitting in a wheelchair beside it, staring at me. She is wearing a loose-weave gray sweater over her nightgown, holding an open purse in her lap. Her hair is in two braids criss-crossed on top of her head. "You! Girly!" she says.

I point to myself, *Me?*

"Yes! Come over here, will you?"

I go to stand in front of her. She crooks her finger, asking me to lean closer. "The nurses stole my wallet again," she says, in a near whisper. "I want you to tell someone. Now, I know the editor of the newspaper, I used to be a reporter there."

I don't know what to say. I smile, start to nod.

"They steal everything," she says. "My socks. My boxes of candy."

"Oh," I say. "Uh huh." Now she's got hold of my arm and doesn't seem to have any intention of letting go.

One of the nurses sees what's happening and comes toward us.

"*Shhhhhh!*" the old lady tells me, her finger up to her lips and spit flying out.

"Now, Theresa," the nurse says. "What are you telling this young lady?"

"I'm telling her the g-d truth!" Theresa says, and drops my arm to point an accusing finger at the nurse. "I'm telling her you nurses *stole* from me again! And she's going to do something about it!"

The nurse smiles at me, then says gently to the old woman, "Tell me what's missing, Theresa."

Theresa stares into space, scowling. She looks like she's chewing her tongue. She has white whiskers growing straight out of her chin, and they look even stranger with all the rouge she has on. Her eyes are blue and watery, full of a kind of angry pain. "I'll tell you what's missing!" she says, finally. She holds up her open purse. "You see a wallet in there? I certainly don't! I certainly *don't.*"

"We have your wallet," the nurse says, and the old lady looks at me. "Ha!" she says. "You see?"

"We have it locked up, as you requested," the nurse says, and the old lady's smile fades. Her knobby fingers grab at the top edges of her sweater, pulling it closer about her.

"Would you like to see it?" the nurse asks.

Theresa snaps her purse shut angrily. "Don't be bothering me with such things! If I want my wallet, I'll ask for it! Stop fussing around me now and get back to work! I never saw such a group of lazy women!"

"Well," I say, "nice meeting you. I have to go."

"Where are you going?" Theresa says. "You only just got here! What kind of visit is this?"

"Well, actually, I—"

"It's all right," the nurse says. "I'll take her for a stroll." She bends down to look into Theresa's face. "How about it? Would you like to go for a little ride?"

Theresa says nothing at first, just stares up into the kind

nurse's face. Then, "Well?" she says. "What's the delay? Giddyap!"

The nurse chuckles softly, then pushes Theresa down the hall.

I head toward Mrs. Randolph's room and find her sitting in a wheelchair, a small floral suitcase beside her. She is dressed in a pair of blue pants and a white blouse with lace on the collar. "Hey, Mrs. Randolph," I say, coming in and sitting on the edge of the bed. I put my back to the woman in the other bed, lying sound asleep and snoring, her mouth wide open like a bottomless pit, no teeth. It's scary to look at her—no offense, but she truly does look like a witch. That pointed chin, those twisted fingers.

"Oh, Katie, what a pleasure to see you. I was afraid I'd miss you."

"No, ma'am." I am trying to act like this is pure normal, but all of a sudden I feel the tragedy of it all. That Mrs. Randolph has been living here, waking up at night to look out of the high little window, where you can't see anything but sky. That her husband is dead. That the thing about people is, we know what we're headed for, and probably we'd rather be like animals, where time is only now and everything is just the greatest because animals never compare anything to anything.

"I'm so glad I'm getting out of here today. Isn't it a madhouse?"

"I did just meet someone pretty strange."

"Pardon?"

I lean closer, tell her again. She smells like baby powder.

"Oh, yes," she says. "There are some real characters in here. But tell me, how are you?"

I start to say fine, then stop.

"Katie?"

I move a chair close to her, so I don't have to shout, and tell her that things are not looking so good at the Bartlett school. That I am worried I won't fit in.

"Oh, don't worry about that," she says. "Everyone feels

strange at first, but then you get to know people. You'll fit in just fine."

"Well, I have already seen that I won't. Believe me. I actually asked if I could just go to my regular school, but my dad won't let me."

Mrs. Randolph's face changes. "What happened?"

I tell her. I tell her about the party and how much I wanted to be a part of those girls. I tell her how I betrayed Cynthia. She says nothing the whole time I'm talking, just nods her head. When I've finished telling her the story, she says, "Well. You've got some problems."

"Yes, ma'am." Maybe I shouldn't have told her.

"But you also have some opportunities."

This feels like the introduction to those pamphlets at the guidance counselors' offices, which never get how anything really is.

"I'll tell you something, Katie. All your life there are going to be defining moments. Turning points, where it will be up to you to decide about something. And your job is always going to be to know what is true for you, what's right, and then to act on it. And you—"

"But I don't always know what's right!" Outside the room, an orderly passes by, whistling the "Aren't You Glad You Use Dial" song. Shut up! I want to say.

"Well, what I believe is that we do always know," Mrs. Randolph says. "But we don't always like to admit it. We become distracted. Seduced. And we make mistakes, we all make mistakes. But deep inside, we always know what's right."

I look down, sigh.

"I also believe you know what to do. And when you're ready, there's no doubt in my mind that you'll do it. I've seen the kind of person you are. I believe in you."

I blink back a million tears. It hurts so strange to have someone be nice to you when you have done something terrible.

"I know I have to ask her to forgive me," I say, and my mouth feels like the dentist has given me Novocain all over.

"Yes, that's true," Mrs. Randolph says. "And you'll have to ask someone else to forgive you, too."

"Who?"

Mrs. Randolph leans forward in the chair a little, resettling herself. Then she says, "You."

I stare at her blankly.

"Before you ask someone else to forgive you, you've got to forgive yourself."

"I don't think I deserve to be forgiven," I say, miserably.

"Well," she says. "As long as you think that, you'll keep yourself from doing anything."

I sit there, thinking. I'm not sure she's right. Finally, I just change the subject and ask her about where she'll be living, and she says it's in a part of the country Henry always loved, South Carolina, and that gets us going in another direction of what is the South really, and who lives there. Texas was one thing; South Carolina is another altogether.

After a few minutes, a tall blond woman comes in the room, her hair in a bun, gold earrings. A navy blue dress, tightly belted, little navy heels. It is Mrs. Randolph's niece, Karen, and she shakes my hand and smiles. She has a soft southern accent, which I love so much. I can see the younger Mrs. Randolph in her face, and it practically kills me dead for so many reasons, and I don't even know what they are.

I go out to the parking lot with them and wave good-bye. I can't believe Mrs. Randolph is really going, but then I can't believe Mr. Randolph is dead either. I wonder if Mrs. Randolph feels like she's going along like in a dream and soon Henry will come back and they'll say, Well, *that* was interesting, now let's go back to our old life.

I sit on the steps to wait for Ginger, imagining what she'll look like as an old lady. And I can see it. Then I try to imagine my father old, and I can see that too. But when I try to think of me as old, it won't work. I just get my inside self saying, *Are you kidding?* The highest age I can go is about twenty. And even that is like science fiction.

I see an older man, dressed in black, getting out of a car and heading for the steps. And then I see that it's Father Compton. I feel my heart speed up, because I know he's come to tell me something terrible. My father got killed. Ginger got killed. They both got killed together.

"Well, hello there, Katie," he says. "What are you doing here?"

Oh, I think. It is just Father Compton, just doing his routine things, saying hello to me. Normal. The word feels like my favorite quilt.

"I was visiting Mrs. Randolph—she just left. She's moving away. What are *you* doing here?"

He sits down beside me, his old bones making him go slow. "Oh, I come once a week to visit a few people. 'Randolph,' you say. Her husband just died recently?"

"Yes."

"Saw it in the paper. I didn't know him."

"He was nice," I say, which of course doesn't even begin to cover it, but then neither would anything else I could say.

Father Compton nods, a little frown of sympathy on his face, and then we just sit there in the sunshine, the breeze blowing so gently now and then, the birds cocking their heads and hop, hop, hopping down the sidewalk in front of us, happy seeming. I can see Father Compton's arm out of the side of my eye, his folded hands, the hair on his knuckles. I guess he is my only friend at the moment. I think of Mrs. Randolph looking at me so serious, telling me I have to forgive myself. Then I think of Mr. Randolph and his suspenders, and the way he looked when he saw his wife with her hair curled. Their living room, with the triangle pillows. Gone, really, even though it is still there. Movers will come soon, Mrs. Randolph told me, to take their things away. Then the house will be empty, and then new people will be there. A little time will pass and then it will seem like the new people have always been there. The way time and situations shift is a mystery of life. The way you can't count on anything staying, that's a sadness. Only yesterday, I saw white hairs in Bones's muzzle. I lay beside him, petting him, feeling so bad that he is getting old. For his part, he just wagged his tail and enjoyed the petting, which is what I mean about animals. They don't pace around, worrying. All they do is say, fine.

A car pulls into the lot—Ginger, coming to get me. So that is the end of our little memorial service, where one of the mourners didn't even know the departed. I stand up, smile good-bye at Father Compton. "Come visit me soon," he tells me, and I say I'll come tomorrow afternoon, if that's all right. Because all of a sudden, I've got an idea.

I HAVE ALWAYS WONDERED WHAT it's like to be inside this confessional. I have seen it from the outside, I once took a look behind the heavy red velvet curtain, and I also once quick tried to look in the part where the priest goes. But that part had a door, and it was locked.

But here I am, kneeling, the real thing, because Father Compton has agreed to do a modified version of a confession for me. The curtain is closed behind me so there is that *whoa!* feeling of being in sacred darkness. Where you kneel there's a velvet cushion so it doesn't hurt too bad, although if you had a lot of sins to talk about, it could get uncomfortable. Which is probably the idea. The priest gets to sit in a chair, because even though he is a sinner too, we are not doing that now. Above the little window you talk through is a crucifix with Jesus looking down. *Well, what have we here?* Like the scientist to the bug.

I looked up at Him for a second, but really, it is not my fault nor that of any of the other people who see Him these days, so I don't see why He has to be hanging there with blood dripping, when He could be shown in heaven with his dad, all happy and risen. Once Ginger asked me about why I went so often to visit a Catholic church when I wasn't Catholic, and I told her it was because of Father Compton, he was like a favorite teacher. And she said good, because Catholics are morbid. Which at first made me think they were like pale-faced vampires, but all she meant was that they seem to have a habit of thinking about the sadness of the world, always reminding you that you are not worthy, not worthy, not worthy. And looking at this crucifix, it does make you wonder.

Now I heard the sound of wood sliding over wood and the whisper of Father Compton. "Okay. Are you ready, Katie?"

"Yes, sir," I say, and it is much too loud. So I whisper, again, "Yes, sir."

"All right. You remember how to start?"

"I do." My heart is beating so fast.

"Anytime you're ready."

I clear my throat. "Okay. So . . . Bless me, Father, for I have sinned."

Really, who talks like this? I feel a little like laughing.

"My sins are the following." And now I don't feel like laughing at all. I cannot say it.

A long time passes. Outside, a car honks. Which seems to prompt Father Compton to say, gently, "Go on."

"I betrayed my best friend," I say, really fast.

"Ah. And how did you do that?"

I stare at the screen between us, covered by what looks like a hanky. Through it, I can see Father Compton's profile, his old head and his bent nose, glasses perched half way down.

"Do I have to say that part? The details?"

"Yes, that would be part of the confession."

I blow some air out of my cheeks and shift my position on the kneeler. The curtain moves and a slim line of light pushes in. Out there in the light is not in here. Out there is freedom. I take in a deep breath, close my eyes. "Okay. Well, it was . . . I was at this party? And I pretended she wasn't really my friend. I talked about her with someone else, and I said I was only with her because I had to be. And I revealed some things about her of a personal nature, which embarrassed her."

"Some things of a personal nature."

"Which I am not telling you no matter what, for one thing I'm not even Catholic, as you know."

"But you know that you embarrassed your friend."

"Yes, because she overheard me."

"I see."

It is too hot in this stupid booth.

"Can you tell me why you did it?"

A long moment. And then I say, "I wanted to make a good impression on the other girl. I wanted her to like me."

"And so to make her like you, you made fun of your friend."

"Yes."

"I wonder if you could tell me why you thought that would make her like you."

I know what he's trying to do. I know exactly. He's saying, Now, what kind of person would want you to make fun of your friend, and why would you want to be involved with anyone like that? But he is a priest and he just doesn't get it. He can't. He is too far away from what real life is like, especially for someone my age. I think back to the night of the party, me in the bathroom with Leigh, her eyes growing wider and wider with what I told her. Her laughing. Finally, I say, "It's just . . . it's how she and her friends are. They make fun of things."

"I see."

"They don't *only* make fun of things! They also . . . They're . . . popular. And they go to great places and they look nice and it's just fun to be with them."

"It's fun to be with them."

When he says it back, it just sounds stupid. And then I think about being with them in the mall. "Well, when I was with them, it wasn't so fun, actually. But I thought it would be."

"You thought you would have fun with them, and it was worth it to betray your friend for that reason." Father Compton has become Father Parrot.

"Yes . . . Well, *no!* I mean, I didn't know she was listening."

"So, if she hadn't been listening, it would have been all right to do."

One thing I will never be is Catholic. It is just too sticky. "It was something I did just at the *moment.* Like I didn't so much think about it. It just seemed like it was the right thing to do at the time."

"But now you feel differently."

"Yes."

"And why is that?"

"Well, because . . . I see now that I shouldn't have made fun of her to try to impress them. Because it hurt her feelings."

"Uh huh."

"And now that she doesn't want to see me, I understand how important she was to me."

"Yes."

He lets that soak in for a while. Then he says, "You know, it's a sad fact that we often take for granted those whom we care about most. But one of the best things about people is that we are able to learn lessons from what we do wrong. I'd like you to think about a few things, Katie. One of those things is, Who else did you betray when you betrayed Cynthia?"

I roll my eyes. "Jesus, I guess."

"Well . . . no, that's not what I was thinking. Although I do believe that when we hurt ourselves, we hurt Him."

"Right." I don't think so. I don't think He watches us so closely. I don't think He watches us at all. If He ever spent even one part of one day watching us, He'd smack His forehead and go right out of business.

"You don't need to answer this question right now. It's just something I'd like you to think about. And you don't need to answer me, you need to answer yourself. Now there's something else I want you to think about, too, which is this: Cynthia is not just Cynthia. Will you think about that? Cynthia is not just Cynthia."

I nod my head, say okay. Maybe Father Compton is getting too old to be doing this. When I get home, I'm making a box of Kraft macaroni and cheese, and I'm going to eat the whole thing out of the big bowl I mix it in. With a big serving spoon.

"I want to give you a penance now, Katie. This is something you do to atone for your sins. What normally happens, is that I give a penance of prayers. But for you . . . Well, how about if you clean the house for your stepmother?"

My eyes widen. One thing Father Compton doesn't know about is how many Venetian blinds we have. And what good will cleaning my own house do? "But . . . shouldn't I just talk to Cynthia?"

"You should do that too, of course. But the penance I've given you is something separate from that. And when you're doing it, I want you to offer it up."

"Pardon me?"

"I want you to offer it up to God."

"The cleaning?"

"Yes."

I think for a while, then say, "No offense, but why in the world would He want that?"

"Well, I believe God cares about all of us. He wants us to learn from our mistakes and move our lives purposefully forward in the right direction. Doing a selfless thing for someone else is a start."

Like Father Compton and God are lying on their beds talking on the phone for hours every night. How does he know what God would like? Cleaning the bathtub and the sink, my usual job, is bad enough. But now I'll have to scrub the toilet. And vacuum. And dust. And the Venetian blinds will take forever. I had to do them once when my mother was sick; Diane did upstairs and I did downstairs. They are so boring to do even when you have music on, and you think you'll crack up before they're done. Do the main part, okay, but then comes the dumb little ends and they *all* have to be dusted on *both* sides. Venetian blinds are what hang in hell, and every day Satan says, "My, my, I see we have some dust again."

But "okay," I say. "I'll do it." My voice is so low, if it were a person it would come up to my knees.

"Good. And now, Katie, I'm going to say a good act of contrition for you. You can just listen."

This is the part you have to watch out for, when the Catholics try to rope you in. I will listen, but I will be well aware of brainwashing techniques.

"Oh, my God, I am heartily sorry for having offended Thee . . ." Father Compton begins. The words are actually kind of pretty, like a poem, and Father Compton reads like he's an actor. When he finishes, I say, "Boy. That was good."

"Your sins are forgiven. Go in peace."

I sit still for a moment. "That's it?"

"Yes."

"Okay, well . . . Thank you!"

"You're welcome."

"Thanks a lot."

"You're welcome."

Forgiven. Just because someone says you are. And yet, millions believe this. For now, I will, too. "Your sins are forgiven. Go in peace." I stand up, and it is a strange and wonderful thing, the lightness inside me.

I wait for Father Compton to leave first, but he doesn't. I guess he's giving me some privacy to make my escape. But I don't leave the church.

I have seen the Catholics kneel at the rail after confession, their rosaries in their hands. I take off the single-pearl necklace Ginger gave me for my last birthday and hold it in my hands. Then I go down the red-carpeted aisle to kneel at the very center of the altar. I put my hands in the tentlike prayer position and let the necklace drape from between my fingers. It feels so pretty, like a ballet pose, and holding it brings a kind of white peace.

There are flowers on the altar, embroidered linens, candlesticks made of gold. Above the altar there is Jesus on the cross again, and off to the side is a statue of his mom, her face full of sad calm. It's comforting looking at Mary, it's like she's saying, Oh listen, don't *I* know how life can be! but of course in a much more elegant way. I look at her face and I hold the necklace tight and I all of a sudden feel a prayer which is too deep and private to be words. It might be able to be music, but never could it be words, as much as I like them. I kneel for a long time, listening to a feeling, which sounds impossible but is not. When I feel the feeling lift and then go away, I stand and start for home.

All along the sidewalk the same trees and houses I passed on the way here look different now. Washed, though there is not a cloud in the sky. Which is blue so pure you think your eyes might be making it up.

M Y GOODNESS!" Ginger exclaims.
"Yes," I say, shyly.
"What have you *done?*"
"I just cleaned up a little."
"A *little!*"

It is Saturday afternoon. My father is playing golf and Ginger has just come back from the hairdresser and the grocery store. Her hair is sprayed stiff like a helmet in the Jackie style; they are going out tonight. She puts two bags on the kitchen counter, her eyes wide and almost crying like Queen for a Day. "It is just *shining* in here!" She turns around slowly, notices the glass full of wildflowers in the center of the table. "And a bouquet!"

"Yes, ma'am."

She comes up to me, smiles, and gives me a big, long hug, which smashes my face bad but you don't want to tell the person. "You didn't have to do this!"

"I wanted to." I check discreetly to see if the cartilage in my nose is still in the same place. Yes.

Ginger sits down at the table, crosses her legs, leans back, and puts her hands behind her head. She looks like Dagwood on the couch, only sitting up. "You know what? I'm going to sit right here and just admire this kitchen."

"Well . . ." I say.

189

"What?"

"Maybe you should look other places. Like the bathroom."

Ginger sits still for a moment, not understanding, and then she smiles like wives do when their husbands hand them a jewelry box–sized present at Christmas. And then she goes down the hall, me right behind her and the dogs right behind me; they know something special is up. Ginger goes into the bathroom and claps her hands together. "Look at this! It's better than Mrs. Webley!"

When Ginger claps her hands, Bones sits down, his ears risen up to alert status. As for Bridgett, she has squeezed past us to sniff around, thinking there must be steak scraps scattered on the floor to cause this much commotion.

"Thank you so much, sweetheart," Ginger says. I feel like moving my foot around on the ground, like TV people just before they say, Aw shucks. Instead, I tell Ginger I have to go to the Wexlers', and I leave her standing in the bathroom. Wait till she notices the Venetian blinds. She will pass out from joy, her mouth a little smile under her X eyes. In my mind's eye I see Father Compton, sitting behind his desk with his fingers laced over his belly, happy and nodding. Maybe God, too. Why not? It seems to me that when it comes to religions, we're all just making it up anyway.

I AM ALMOST ASLEEP WHEN THE PHONE RINGS, waking me up. I look at the clock: ten thirty. I guess my father and Ginger are still out; no one is answering.

I go out into the hall, pick up the phone. "Hello?"

"Katie?"

It is Mrs. O'Connell.

I sit on the floor, my back against the wall. "Yes?" I should have said, Yes, ma'am.

"Is Cynthia with you?"

". . . No."

"Well, I wonder if you know where she is."

"No. No, ma'am, I don't."

She sighs, impatient. "Well, I just don't . . . She's been gone since after dinner. I didn't even know she'd left. We had an argument, and she . . . Katie, do you think you could help me find her?"

I stand up. "I'll ride my bike over."

"No. I'll come and get you."

I pull on my jeans and a blouse, write a quick note to my father, and wait at the door. When I see the shine of headlights I run to the driveway and climb in Mrs. O'Connell's car.

She doesn't look at me. But she says, "Thank you," and I say, "It's okay."

WE START BY DRIVING UP and down the streets of Cynthia's neighborhood. Mrs. O'Connell said Cynthia took her bike, so we go for several miles in every direction. Neither of us sees anything.

Finally, Mrs. O'Connell pulls off at the side of one of the streets. "I'm going to have to go back and tell her father. We'll have to call the police. He doesn't even know she's gone. He's working in his office down in the basement. I told him I was running out to the all-night market to buy milk." She turns to me, stares for a long moment. She starts to say something, then stops.

"I know," I say, and I think I do know. I think what she wants to say is how much she loves Cynthia, how she couldn't stand it if anything has happened to her, how much she regrets having done anything that might have caused Cynthia to leave. If that's what she's saying, I know how she feels.

She puts the car in gear, starts driving again.

I look out the window, wonder about how this has come to be, that I am driving around in the dark with Cynthia's mother, looking for her. I wonder what happened that Cynthia ran off like this. I wonder if she got so angry she felt like killing her mother again. And then, suddenly, I know where she is. I even think I know how she is sitting, her head resting on her folded arms. "You know, there's one more place we can try," I say.

Mrs. O'Connell looks over at me, hope.

"But you can't come. I'll tell you where to take me, but you'll have to wait in the car."

"I will."

I can't believe it. She agrees, just like that. No questions asked. Except for one. "Which way?" she asks, and I tell her.

CYNTHIA IS AT THE HILL, just as I suspected. She is not sitting like I thought, though. Instead, she is standing, her back to me. When I call her name she jumps, then turns around quickly.

"I'm sorry," I say. "I didn't mean to scare you."

She says nothing.

"Your mom is worried about you. We were driving around, looking for you."

Again, nothing.

"She called to see if you were with me. I said I'd help her look. I thought you might be here. Are you thinking about the fight you had with her?"

Cynthia just stares at me.

I swallow. "Or about the fight we had?"

She looks away from me, rubs one arm with the other.

"Cynthia? Are you going to talk to me?"

She doesn't answer. There is nothing that makes you feel stupider than when someone won't acknowledge the fact that you're talking to them. Everything you say sounds so ridiculous.

"I just want you to know I'm so sorry about the things I said about you. I don't know why I did it."

Nothing.

"Well, actually, I guess I do know."

She won't look at me, but I can tell she's listening.

"It was because I wanted to be friends with them. I wanted to be popular, and I thought if I were friends with them, I would be. You know how we always talk about being popular, how good it would feel."

Nothing.

"Right?"

She sighs, the tiniest sound.

"I guess doing that to you is one of the dumbest things I've ever done. I wish I could undo it, but I can't. So I wish we could at least talk about it. Could we?"

Nothing. It is so quiet I swear I can hear my watch ticking on my arm. "Cynthia? I want you to know I didn't tell your mother where the hill is. She's a block away. I'll take you to her if you want."

She takes a step toward me, then stops. "Listen, Katie, I have to tell you something. I don't think I can ever forgive you. I've thought about it a lot. I don't think I want to see you anymore, ever."

I swallow, nod. "This way," I say, and start walking. Once I turn around to look at her to see if she has changed her mind. But she stares straight ahead, wheeling her bike beside her, not seeing me. Not wanting to.

I AM THE STUDENT AND HENRY IS MISS LINDA. This is his latest. He is Miss Linda, the school teacher, dressed in an apron and with a scarf draped over his head, and I must sit on the stairs and answer his questions. When I get one right, I can advance a step up. When I get one wrong, I must come down one. Henry thinks he is hysterical, and so do his brothers. They wanted to put lipstick and rouge on him, but he wouldn't let them. But he doesn't mind talking in his high, lady voice and keeping one hand on his hip and wearing his mother's big rhinestone clip-on earrings. His brothers won't be students, but they sit on the hall floor watching, cheering if I miss an answer and booing if I get one right. So far the only ones I've missed are baseball questions. As if I would know Roger Maris's batting average. I have made up a rule that there can be no more sports questions, so the game should be over soon.

"How many feet are in a mile?" Henry asks.

"Five thousand, two hundred, and eighty," I say. A step up.

"How many planets?"

"Nine."

"Which one is closest to the sun?"

"Mercury." Two more steps to go.

"How do dogs air-condition themselves?"

"By panting."

"Baby questions!" Mark says. And he comes up to whisper in Henry's ear.

"Do snakes have lungs?" Henry asks, and I say, No, because of course not.

"Wrong!" Henry says, and I sit still for minute, then say, "Show me."

"No way," David says. "She's trying to cheat."

"I am not," I say. "I'll stay right here. You show me where it says snakes have lungs."

They stand there, thinking, and then there is the sound of a car horn. Their parents are home. Everything is so different between the Wexlers now. At first Mrs. Wexler acted sort of shy and guilty, but now she is just better. She looks like she had a good long nap.

Henry quick takes off his costume, handing the earrings to me to put back on his mother's dresser. The best part of baby-sitting is when the parents come home and you can just be a kid again. Who gets paid and then walks out the door, free.

A T KEVIL'S JEWELERS is a pair of beautiful earrings which I believe are opals. They have a milky sheen that changes from blue to pink and they would look good with anything, jeans to a frilly white formal. I have enough money saved to buy them. But first I am just staring at them with the stomachache of longing, as I have so often done. This makes the buying better.

"May I help you?" the salesman asks. He is a tall, thin, older man, who has a smile that is like a little frown below a nose that is smelling something bad. He thinks I'm just that annoying girl again, getting fingerprints all over his case. Imagine his surprise when I tell him I want to buy those earrings and that I have all the cash right here in an envelope in my purse.

"Yes," I say. "I would like to make a purchase."

"I see. And what is it that you would you like to buy?"

I point to the earrings. "Those, right there."

He pulls them from the case and shows them to me, but he holds them so I won't touch. He sniffs, not the kind like when you have a cold, but the kind when you are just a snob. "These are rather expensive."

"I know exactly how much they are. I'll take them."

"Well!" He is so pleased with himself, although he has done nothing. He puts the earrings in a box. "Any gift wrap?"

I start to say no, but then I think *Why not?* "Yes, please," I say.

This will be a present from me to me. I will leave the earrings on my desk to look at for one week, and then I will open them. "Why, thank you!" I will say to myself.

"Don't mention it," I will answer.

"Why don't you try them on?" I'll say.

"Don't mind if I do," I'll answer, and then regard myself in the mirror, Grace Kelly.

"Pink paper or white?" the man asks.

"Pink," I say. Which is Cynthia's favorite color. And the idea that I guess has been there all along steps out from behind the bushes. Surprise, it says.

WHEN I GET HOME, I pull the phone as far as it will go, which is not far. I dial Cynthia's number, then pull the receiver into my bedroom and close the door on the cord.

"Hello?"

Thank goodness, at last it is Cynthia herself.

"Hi," I say. "It's me."

Silence.

"It's Katie."

"I *know*."

"I was wondering if we could get together for just a minute," I say.

"I told you, I—"

"Just for a minute. Suppose I come over after dinner, some time around—"

"Can't."

My stomach does a little flash of anger. "You mean you don't want to."

"Even if I did want to, I couldn't. Tonight is Girl Scouts, your favorite."

"Well," I say, and nothing else comes to me to say.

"Okay, so . . .'Bye."

"*Wait*. Cynthia. Are you just always going to say no when I call you? Can't we just get together and talk? I'm *sorry*, okay? I'm really sorry. I just want to—"

"I don't want to be your friend anymore, Katie. It's just too . . . I don't want to. I don't feel like I could ever trust you again. And anyway, we won't really be seeing each other anymore, you'll be going to a new school, with new friends."

"They're not my friends."

"That's funny. It sure didn't seem like that."

"But see, that's why I want to get together. I just want to explain."

I hear a car door slam. Ginger, home from wherever she was. I speak quickly. "Let's just make a time to get together, how about tomorrow night we go to a movie or something?"

"I'm sorry, Katie, but no."

"Come *on,* Cynthia!"

"I have to go."

She hangs up. I can't believe it. I lie on the floor, the phone against my chest. I hear Ginger calling me and I want to roar at her like a monster.

Instead, I come into the hall, put the phone back, and then go out into the kitchen, where Ginger is getting things out of the refrigerator, getting ready to make dinner. "Leigh called while you were gone," Ginger says. "She wanted to know if it would be all right if she dropped by."

I shrug.

"I told her yes; I hope that's all right."

"I guess."

"Katie?"

"I'm just going to take a walk," I say. "I'll be home for dinner."

Hearing me say the word "walk," the dogs look up hopefully. I might as well bring them—all you do is put their leashes on and they act like they've won the sweepstakes. They're lucky they can't talk. All they ever do wrong to each other is bite, and then presto, it's over.

I WALK FAR OUT INTO THE FIELDS, then let the dogs loose. They get busy right away, sniffing everything, running around. I wonder what they smell. You can tell the scents are all different: Sometimes they just take a little whiff and keep on running; other times they stop dead in their tracks and sniff forever. And sometimes they sniff very delicately, their lips drawn back a bit, as though they're saying, *Ewww, this smells* awful, *let me smell it some more*. That's something about dogs you have to accept: The worse it smells, the better they like it, and they will roll in it if you let them. When you have bad breath they want to kiss you.

I sit in some long grass, watch for a while to see if I can find some ants working. The thing about watching ants is, you see some order and elegance to the whole works. And also is it a time of you wondering who is higher, really.

But there are no ants. There are no grasshoppers, either. There is just me and the thought of Cynthia. Thinking of her used to be a comfort and now it is a problem. How will I ever solve this? Maybe there are things too big to say sorry for.

When I was about five, my mother read me a story about a little girl who had a bracelet that told her when she was thinking about doing a wrong thing. It would stick her like a pin, and then she would know not to do it. I used to wish I had a bracelet like that, because I was so interested in doing the right thing. I was a very sincere little kid. And then I grew into the me I am now, and now feels like I am at a carnival of dazzling lights and rides and barkers making all false promises that sometimes I can't help believing. If, on the night of the party, I'd had a bracelet like in the story, it would have been sticking me like a porcupine. But what's really scary is, I think I would have ignored the pain. Or I would have taken the bracelet off, *Never mind, I'll handle this*.

For the first time, I let myself fully imagine what it must have been like for Cynthia to hear me say those things. How she must have come up to the bathroom door all happy and excited like she'd been, and then she heard me say I had to bring her, and then she heard me say the rest. She must have felt so embarrassed and also panicked to look around and see that she was stuck there. And the thought of her own house, even with her crazy mother, must have seemed so comforting. I think of the dignified way she asked to use the phone, the straightness of her back going up those basement stairs, and I think of how I watched her go. I remember now so clearly what I was thinking. I was saying to myself, Oh well, I'll lose her but look who I'll have instead. And even though Father Compton has said my sins are forgiven, I know they're not really. Because I didn't say the biggest sin, which is this: Not only do I feel bad about Cynthia getting hurt, I also feel bad because I don't belong to that group any more than she does. What if they *had* accepted me in the real way? Would I still have wanted to be friends with Cynthia, even part-time? I wonder. And in my unsureness is such shame.

I rest my head against my raised knees, searching for the warm salt smell of skin. I find it, but it does not provide the comfort it usually does. It comes to me that I have hurt myself along with Cynthia, and that is what Father Compton meant when he asked who else did I betray. Inside me was the shimmering truth of how I really am and what I really believe, but I acted against it without even thinking, and now it does not shimmer so much. Now it is dark and hard to find. When you realize that for your whole life you will have to be so careful making choices, it can make you feel tired. That is certainly how I feel; I am just so tired.

I lie down, then turn my head to look at the grass. I used to do this and pretend I was in the jungle, the grass so high it towered over me. I could hear the drums of the natives passing on some dark, urgent message, and the wild rhythm made my blood jump. Now it doesn't work anymore. I am in Missouri, and the grass only looks tall because I am lying down.

But. Look here. On a blade of grass right in front of me is an ant. Carrying something on his back that looks way too big for him. But there he goes, doing his job without wasting any time. Every day he does this, whether anyone is watching him or not. Every day he makes a Herculean effort and offers not one word of complaint.

I stand up and whistle for the dogs. Too soft. I try whistling with my fingers in my mouth, something I've been trying to do for years. Lo and behold, it works. The dogs run to me. My wish is their command. I am Captain Katie, in charge of my own life.

WHEN I GET HOME, I see Leigh's car in the driveway, her mother sitting in the front seat, waiting for her. And then the front door opens, and Leigh comes out, spots me coming down the road. She holds up her hand to wave, says something to her mom as she passes the car, then comes out into the street to meet me.

"Hi!" she says, all like a cheerleader. She flashes her gorgeous smile.

"Hi."

"Are these your dogs?"

"Yeah." I pull back on the leashes; they'd like very much to sniff Leigh to death.

She reaches down to pet Bones. "I just met your stepmother."

I look up to the house to see if Ginger is looking out. No sign of her.

"She's so *adorable*. And so's your little *house*."

I start to say thanks, then don't.

Leigh looks at her watch. "I have to go. But I brought you something, Katie. I'm going to be running for class president and I want to get going on posters so they'll all be done when school starts. I brought you a sample and some supplies—just make them like the sample."

"I'm sorry. I don't think I have time."

Leigh stands there, blinks once. Twice. Then she says, "Well, we're *all* doing them."

"That's good. Probably then you'll have enough help without me."

She smiles, confused. And behind her confusion is her anger.

"And now *I* have to go," I say.

"Well, if you're not going to help, I'm going to take the poster board back," Leigh says.

"Okay."

She sighs. "Are you *sure* you can't do some?"

I know exactly what she's asking. "Yeah, I'm sure," I say.

She raises an eyebrow, then spins around and walks ahead of me toward the house to get her things. I slow down so she'll be out by the time I go in.

AFTER DINNER I LIE ON MY BED holding a pillow to my chest. I am thinking about Father Compton saying, "Cynthia is not just Cynthia," and I think I know now what he means. She stands for something. For many things.

I look at my watch. Seven o'clock. She'll be just starting the Girl Scout meeting. She'll be sitting there wearing her uniform, and her mother will be all excited and acting like a jerk. Cynthia will go along with whatever they're doing. I've heard Girl Scouts make planters from tin cans, purses from the plastic boxes strawberries come in. *Oh, Cynthia*, I think, and feel so bad for her.

I go over to my desk, pull out the letter from Cherylanne I got yesterday, reread the last page.

> *One thing that I am thinking so much about lately is how fast something big in your life can happen. How you don't even know sometimes that you're making a choice when you are. Now I am going to be a mother when I thought I would be who knows what after senior year. I want my baby and I know I will be a good mother, but it is something strange that so many other options are no longer available to me. Not to be like a movie star, but they are gone with the wind. I think about you a lot Katie, and only last night I was on the back steps thinking of how we used to drink pickle juice, which I don't care I still say is a*

good treat on a hot summer day and also scientific because it gives you back salt. I guess we never will do that again. Sometimes I think of how at the very instant you think now it is over. I mean that moment. I guess all you can do is look forward or you'll drive yourself crazy.

Another girl name I am thinking of is Katherine. Which guess why, as if you didn't know. The names are up to me because I asked Darren again what if it's a girl and he said "I have no idea," all flat and staring out the windshield straight ahead. "I have no idea" is also his brilliant suggestion if it's a boy.

I am glad we write to each other. It is like a hand to hold and don't think I don't know how important that is. Especially when my other friends like CAROLYN DELANEY and SHERRY DUTTON and EVERYONE ELSE have shown their true colors. Of black. Their hands are nowhere to be found except covering their mouths as they talk about me, their favorite hobby. One thing to say about you, Katie, is that you are true. You should be proud of it, and don't ever let anyone tell you otherwise.

I fold the letter up, put it back in the drawer. She is wrong. I am not true. I only used to be. I sigh. There is Cherylanne, in Texas. Here am I, in Missouri. And Cynthia is in a Girl Scout meeting a few blocks away, yet she is farther from me than Cherylanne. I wonder if she misses me at all.

I go to my closet to get out my robe. I'm just going to get in my pajamas and read myself to sleep, I don't care how early it is. On the floor of the closet, I see the Girl Scout manual Cynthia's mother gave me. I take it over to my desk, open to the first page. In the introduction, they ask if you know about Anna Shaw, the American pioneer girl who became a preacher and a doctor. And do you know about Marie Curie and Florence Nightingale. They tell you about Phyllis Wheatley, the first Negro poet in America, whose poetry was praised by George Washington. I never even heard of Phyllis Wheatley or Anna Shaw. It makes you feel odd to know you can learn something from something you made fun of.

I look through the rest of the manual. Here is something about Sacajawea, who was an Indian guide and interpreter for the Lewis and Clark expedition. She could read the sun, the stars and the trees. And here is Louisa Alcott, whose writing helped provide for her family. Amelia Earhart was a gardener and liked dress designing; she made her own clothes. Knowing that seems to make her more 3-D.

There is stuff in the manual about how to eat, how to have good hygiene, how to nurse someone who is ill, how to silk-screen and tie-dye, how to row a boat or pitch a tent or determine map distances. There is information about turtles and tadpoles, something that says that if your pet understands and responds to ten words, he is very smart. You can tell birds by their nests. The General Assembly of the United Nations has five parts to it. Three dots is S in Morse Code. All snakes have teeth. And here is something astounding: The needle on a compass does not point to the North Pole. Instead, it points to the magnetic deposit known as the magnetic North Pole, fifteen hundred miles away from the true North Pole. If you live in Portland, Oregon, the needle points 22 degrees east of north. In Portland, Maine, it points 15 degrees west. So you have to factor in the variation if you want to find the true direction. This is one of those scientific facts that you run through your brain and you feel awe, but then you run it through your heart and it's like music. Because it is about everything.

In the back are all the badges you can earn: Salt Water Life, Folk Dancer, Wood, Glass, Pottery. Handywoman, First Aid, and Adventurer. Garden Flower, Wild Plant, and, I swear, Cat and Dog. One badge shows the most beautiful insect, with butterflylike wings and a beautiful, segmented, arching-up tail. "Swimmer" has a curled wave and two seagulls, and "Dancer" has a foot with a ballet slipper and a wing at its heel. There are badges for Reader and Puppeteer, Aviation and Traveler. For Farmer and Homemaker and Cook and Adventurer and First Aid to Animals. And here is one with a picture of a scroll, with words written on it. It is the badge for Writer, and to earn it one of the things to do is to write a poem.

I think of how once I was standing in a church on Christmas Eve. There was a spicy scent of pine in the air, candles glowed, and there was baby Jesus in a crèche on the altar. There was a sermon about love and joy, about redemption. And then everyone began to sing "O Holy Night." Next to me was a woman who could not carry a tune. At first I was so annoyed, listening to her. I wondered, *Why does she sing so loud when she doesn't even know how?* Then I looked at her and she was so pure, staring straight ahead, her face lit from within. Something moved into my heart at that moment that I did not really understand, but I understand it now: It is never about how good your voice is; it is only about feeling the urge to sing, and then having the courage to do it with the voice you are given. It is about what people try to share with each other, even if so many of us are so off-key when we do it. It is about saying we are some- where, when what we mean is we are as close as we are able to get.

I go back to my closet, find the uniform Mrs. O'Connell gave me, and put it on. It's not so bad.

THIS IS WHAT I THOUGHT WOULD HAPPEN: I thought I would knock on the door and Cynthia would answer. Behind her, her mother would be standing with her arms crossed, unsure as to my intentions. Cynthia would hesitate, but then she would stand aside and I would step in. Without a word, Cynthia and I would walk down the hall and into her room. She would close the door and sit on the bed expectantly and not say a word, which would be her right. I would stand before her. I would start with a little joke about the uniform, like, "So what do you think, is it me?" She would smile and look down in her lap. I would be looking around the room a little, so grateful to be back. Then I would sit down beside her and say, "Cynthia, I want to tell you again how very sorry I am for what I said. I made a bad mistake. I was trying to get in with those girls and it was at your expense. I know it may take some time, but I hope you can forgive me, because I really care about you and now I see who my true friends are, and also I see what really matters to me." She would start crying a little and so would I. I would give her the earrings, and we would hug, and just then her mother would knock on the door and say, "Time for the meeting, girls." And Cynthia would put on the earrings and we would go out to the living room. And it would still be dumb, but this time I would be able to see the good mixed in.

Here is what did happen: On the way over, a car full of guys passed me. They slowed down and started hooting and laughing. I think it was the beret. I ignored them and finally they peeled out and left. When I got to Cynthia's, she answered the door, just like I thought she would. But she did not let me in. She just looked a little irritated and said, "Katie, I said *no*," and shut the door. I couldn't believe it. She didn't say anything about the uniform. I stood there for a while, and then the door opened again. It was Mrs. O'Connell saying, "I'm sorry, Katie, I guess you're going to have to leave." I nodded okay, and started walking home. I wished so much for darkness. My whole face ached from wanting to cry.

When I walked in, my father lowered the newspaper to look at me, and Ginger said, "Is the meeting over already?" I nodded and went straight back to my room and took off the uniform and put on my pajamas. I went to my desk and took out some paper and a pen and started a letter to Cynthia. Here is how far I got: "Dear Cynthia." There was nothing more to say. I have said all I could, the ball is in her court, as they say, and she does not want to play.

Then I tried to write a poem and I could not write anything. I sat for so long, holding my pen, and then finally I put it down.

Now I lean back in my chair and think about how high above us are so many millions of stars. And how the moon is always changing phases. And how, when you lie outside on your back and give yourself over to the heavens, you wonder why people aren't wiser than they are. But then you get up and come in the house and just keep making mistakes like everybody else.

I pick up the present I was going to give to Cynthia and start to open it, then don't. Instead, I put it in my closet, way in the back.

I AM THE REPORTER AND MARK IS THE VAMPIRE. Henry is the corpse, lying outside under a tree with two fang marks made with Mrs. Wexler's laundry marker. It is such a hot day I can hardly move, and I wish I could play the corpse, it would be easy as pie. David is the good guy who is not in the movie yet; he is sitting off to the side wetting himself down with a squirt gun.

I am examining Henry and writing things in a notebook, and Mark is somewhere behind me, getting ready to pounce. Then I am supposed to look up at him and scream, then faint. At which point David will spring out and wrestle with the vampire. We don't know yet who will win.

I write in my notebook as I think a real reporter would: "Corpse is a young male, about seven years of age. Parallel holes at side of neck suggest vampire activity." I feel a hand on my shoulder and I turn around, prepared to scream. But it is not Mark with his black cape safety pinned to his T-shirt. It is Cynthia.

"Oh," I say, like a dope.

"Hi," she says.

"Want to play?" Henry asks. "Hey, do you want to play?"

She shrugs. "Okay."

"You're *dead*, Henry!" Mark says, coming out from behind the bushes. "Shut up!"

"Yeah, but can she play?" Henry asks.

Mark stands sullenly, scratching his arm. He has Franco-American spaghetti stains at the sides of his mouth, and at the back of his head is a little dent from where Mrs. Wexler had to cut gum out of his hair. "Fine" he says. "But now we'll have to go all the way back to the beginning."

"Who do you want to be?" I ask Cynthia, holding back a feeling like tears and laughter mixed.

"I don't know," she says. "Myself?"

"That would be good," I say. "Maybe I'll be that, too."

She nods, just a little at first, and then harder, smiling.

A big breeze rises up and shakes the branches of the trees. The leaves rustle violently, then settle back down into calm greenness, as though nothing has happened. I think when I get home, I'll sit at my desk and find a way to make something of that.